STUART BRAY

Cotton Candy

First published by Static Publishing 2022

This novel is entirely a work of fiction. The names, characters and incidents portrayed in it are the work of the author's imagination. Any resemblance to actual persons, living or dead, events or localities is entirely coincidental.

First edition

ISBN: 9798446458202

Editing by Jason Nickey

This book was professionally typeset on Reedsy.
Find out more at reedsy.com

Contents

Acknowledgement

Thank you to all my readers... you are the reason I keep this crazy train rolling.

Thank you, Nana, for letting me borrow so many of those books when I was younger, you are the reason this was a dream in the first place.

Thank you Faja for always being a great friend and dad at the same time.

Check out these other titles form Static Publishing
    The Heretic (2016)
    Every little flaw (2022)
    Broken pieces of June (2022)

This book contains extremely graphic violence and strong language that some readers may find offensive.

Readers 18+ highly recommended

PROLOGUE

Felching (sucking or eating semen out of someone's anus) is a sexual behavior about which virtually nothing has been written in the scholarly literature, despite the fact that it appears to be a not-uncommon practice among certain subpopulations of men who have sex with men (MSM).

The lights flashed as I ran through the crowd of bystanders, my asshole bled profusely.

"Move! Get out of here!"

I shoved passed the smiling families, they held their children's hands tightly, even more so when a nude, bloody twink shoved past them dazed from morphine.

"What the fuck is your problem pervert? There are kids all over the place and you are running around like that?"

I could not see the angry father who was shouting at me, I was too preoccupied with getting as far from this place as I could. My mangled asshole felt as if someone had squeezed a lemon on it, the pain was worth it, I had to escape.

"There you are, Gavin"

One of the clowns stepped in my path; his arms reached out to me like a monster in a child's nightmare.

"Get the hell away from me!" I tried to scream but my face was just so damn numb, the morphine would wear off eventually.

1

I stumbled to the left, avoiding the clown's grasp.

"You get back here you fucking twink bitch!" the clown growled loudly behind me.

There were more of them around here somewhere, they were hiding amongst the flashing lights, the rattling of the rides, they even hid within the sweet smell of the cotton candy.

"Gavin" a voice whispered from the crowd.

The crowd of families had moved far away from me, leaving me an open target next to the Ferris Wheel.

"I didn't want any of this!" drool dripped like honey from the sides of my mouth. "Leave me the fuck alone!" I screamed as loud as I could. I am not sure if I screamed it before or after I fell face first in the damp grass.

"We are going to take good care of you" the group of clowns circled above me, their gloved white hands pulling me in every direction.

"Wake the fuck up cunt! You are punching my fucking back!" the man on the top bunk shouted in a raspy, worn-out voice.

"I was having the craziest dream" I sighed, wiping the sweat from my forehead.

"Yeah, we all heard your bad dream, you fucking twink prick! You woke everyone up. If you think about having another one of your faggot-ass dreams, make sure you do it behind the dumpster outside!" the man coughed and wheezed like his rant took all the oxygen from his body.

"Sorry about that, it won't happen again" I said rolling over on my side to stare at the cold brick wall.

I wondered how many other people I had woken up. I looked around the room, but it was too dark to tell. The mattress creaked under my weight. It was not the most comfortable sleep I had had, but it was at least indoors. Going back to sleep was not an option at this point, these goddamned nightmares were becoming more and more frequent. There was no peace to be found in this life awake or asleep, everything was a nightmare that left me screaming myself awake.

CHAPTER 1: THE BALLAD OF GAVIN WHITE

Moon City, 1998

"You all need to clear the fuck out, this isn't the four seasons, we have a shit ton more of you bums that need a bed for the night"

Patrick ran the shelter; he had a big mouth with an even bigger temper. He walked down the cluttered aisle of bunkbeds, kicking them obnoxiously.

"You can't suck another night out of me, Pinky. You got to fuck off with the rest!"

I shook my head not paying much attention to him as he stood just a few inches from me. I was not supposed to even have a bed last night. Apparently, the shelter was over capacity, and I had to take a load in the mouth just to get a decent night's sleep.

"Come back in a few days and I'll have the hammer waiting for those cute little faggot lips" Patrick laughed as he continued down the aisle. I had heard it all before, the names did not bother me anymore, they hadn't in a long time.

Calling myself an easy target due to my own life choices, plus a few that were not exactly any fault of my own was the understatement of the century.

The pink dye in my previously blonde hair seemed to never wash out. Even when I would sneak in those hotel rooms for the night to use the shower, I could never get this fucking color out. I was around six feet, give or take an

3

inch, and skinny enough to hide behind a street sign. I looked like a skeleton painted a shade of peach.

"Hey, my cousin is supposed to be staying here tonight. You could probably suck his dick for his spot." I looked up at the toothless old man hanging his head from the bunk above me.

"I appreciate the offer, but I've sucked enough dirty dicks this week" I replied with a sigh.

"Suit yourself queer" the old man's head disappeared.

This must be the most awkward time period to be gay, I was called faggot or homo more than my own name.

"Come on you lazy fucks, I need you to hit the bricks so this place can be cleaned up, there's oatmeal in the main hall, grab a bowl and fuck off!" Patrick's face was more flustered than usual, he was not one of those people that opened a homeless shelter because deep down he was a good person, he opened it to receive a fat check from the city every month, plus run his own prostitution ring out of the basement.

Outside was as gray as usual, a city stuck in a 1960's sitcom. The slightly cool breeze blew a waded-up newspaper through the alley like urban tumbleweeds.

"Depressing isn't it?" a voice startled me. "Fucking place looks like something Bob Ross would see in his nightmares."

I turned slightly to see the man I assumed was talking to me but noticed he was looking up at the clouds, his eyes squinted like the sun was about to burst from behind the toxic balls of fluff floating low in the sky.

"Yeah, it's hard to remember a time this city had any color at all." The man looked over at me as if he were surprised someone had heard him.

"You lived here long pal?" he asked turning his body in my direction.

He was an older man, the wrinkles on his light clay colored face looked like they were made softly with a sharp razorblade. His frizzled white hair hung in random strands from beneath the faded black toboggan resting atop of his head, he had the bluest fucking eyes I had ever seen.

"I don't remember a time I didn't live here" I said making quick eye contact

4

and then turning away to flip the collar on my jacket, hoping to stop the breeze from hitting my neck.

"This place is like the twilight zone on a good day" the old man said with a chuckle.

I had never seen this man before. I had been coming here for so long and had seen a hundred different faces. I feel as if I would have remembered this one, especially one with eyes as blue as his.

"You been coming here long Mr.?" I extended my hand; he wrapped his around it with a soft grip.

"You can call me Raguel" he said smiling.

His eyes were so blue that it became extremely difficult to turn away from once you looked for too long, it was like gazing into another galaxy.

"Well Raguel, it was a pleasure to meet you" I shot one last quick smile as I turned and started down the ally.

Shit, was it rude of me to just spout a quick goodbye and leave without allowing him to respond? I turned to look back at the old man, half expecting him to be giving me some dirty look.

"What the hell?" I asked myself aloud.

The old man was gone, no way did he scurry away in the time it took me to walk five feet. I looked around at the rest of societies burden that were pouring out of the exit, and he was nowhere in sight. I shrugged my shoulders, I had more important things I needed to worry about at this point.

"Well would you look who decided to show his face" an all too familiar voice called out a few yards ahead of me.

I looked up at the dark-purple Cadillac that was irresponsibly parked at the end of the ally. "You have something for me you pink haired mother fucker?" Lonzo was what the average onlooker would call a pimp. "You are hiding out in some fucking shelter like a homeless fucking slob? That makes you look like garbage, and in turn that makes me look like a garbage man. Do I look like I collect trash pinky? Do you earn like shit for weeks and then hide away like a beaten gay mutt? I feed you hoes good every night. Do these nasty mother fuckers feed you better up in this bitch?"

5

I could not see those dark intense eyes that were kept hidden away under cheap, dark sunglasses. I felt like a child who had been caught doing something I was not supposed to, a deer in bright headlights on a dimly lit country road.

"I just needed a place to stay last night" I stammered; his stern expression never changed.

"When you need a place to sleep you stay with the rest of the product. You sleep with the merchandise"

He pointed a long coke nail at me like a loaded pistol. His purple fur jacket looked as if someone had hunted down and skinned something from a Dr. Seuss book. It matched his white pinstriped suit.

"I know I should have slept at the house, I just needed to get away for a night, needed a change of scenery." I pleaded pathetically.

The house that Lonzo was referring to was an old run-down shit hole that he rented a few years back that he allowed his 'Merchandise' to live and sleep in when they weren't pulling tricks. Lonzo only pimped male prostitutes, he said that a skinny little twink was every trick's secret pleasure.

"Nobody sucks dick like a desperate faggot" he said the first time I met him. Lonzo himself was gay, though he would never admit it. I had seen him getting his ass hole eaten by one of the houses twinks named Jordan, another was laying on his back with Lonzo's uncircumcised black cock in his mouth.

"Why would a mother fucker like you need a change of scenery? A house full of your fellow degenerate fuck holes not up to your high standards? You are not even a top earner, you're a cheap chili ring for a white trash cock."

Lonzo was a professional at completely degrading the people around him. I thought back to how much I hated living in that disgusting house. The house that should have been legally condemned by this point. Everyone that slept and shit there were all the stereotypical queers that were overly flamboyant, the ones who would dress in women's clothing while still having a five o'clock shadow. They would tilt their skinny little wrists and talk shit about the tricks they had sucked off the night before. I fucking hated them all.

"I'm sorry, Lonzo. I'll stay at the house from now on, and I'll start earning better." I felt defeated, just a few simple insults and a blow to my already meaningless existence and I was down for the count.

"Well pinky, I'm sure glad you've come to your senses... but I can't let you just come back around my house of fuck meat, giving them ideas that they can just leave whenever they damn well please. I'm going to need to make an example out of you now. If you don't start earning real quick, I'll be sure to make even more of example out of your worthless ass."

My skin crawled as he lifted his right hand up to slightly lower his sunglasses. His eyes were an endless black, it felt like I was going to suddenly fall into them and be lost in the darkest part of space.

"You don't have to do that Lonzo, I learned my lesson. It won't happen again, I swear I'll start doing better, I'll hustle more tricks."

I was almost tempted to put my hands up as if I were praying for his mercy. WHACK!

A smack to the back of my head made the tall buildings around me spin like the washing machines I would watch sitting next to my mother as a kid on a Sunday afternoon at the laundromat.

Instinctively, I put my hands out to brace my fall to the asphalt. The hard ground stopped me so suddenly that I could feel my head snap back so far, I headbutted the top of my spine. A sharp kick to the ribs sent the little air I had left right out of my body.

"Work his ass over in places the other faggots will notice, dumb fuck."

I heard Lonzo barking orders at his two mafia looking henchmen. I could not quite remember their names. They were twin brothers with the stereotypical henchmen leather jackets and black sunglasses.

"Get him up where I can see his pretty face." Lonzo shouted as he stomped his shiny white loafers on the pavement.

"Come here cutie" one of the henchmen whispered in my ear as he pulled me up by my hair.

I knew there was a crowd of people staring down the alley at the ass beating I was graciously given What were they going to do? Lonzo was a feared name in the area, no one would question why some fag was getting smacked around.

"You know your place now, pinky? You gonna earn me some fucking money tonight bitch?"

I was forced face to face with Lonzo, the halitosis was unbearable but impossible to turn away from at this moment. "Are you going to get your ass back to the house after you clean the cum out of your ass tonight? or am I going to have to throw you in the trunk like a sack of groceries?" he asked with a smile that showed off the gaudy gold tooth that he was so proud of.

"I'll be there Lonzo, and I swear I'll earn big tonight" I pleaded in the way that made him feel like a big man.

"That's a good bitch" he said, patting me on the head like a newly trained dog.

After Lonzo and his goons sped off down the road, I leaned against the side of a building, holding my ribs like they were about to fall out. The onlookers had gone on about their business like it was just another day. I finally found the strength to pull myself to my feet, a bit wobbly but stable enough to walk. The stench of week-old garbage danced around my nostrils like smells did in cartoons. This city was an absolute cesspool, it needed to be condemned, then bulldozed for good measure. Walking down the sidewalk, looking around at all the faces buried under dirty blankets or bundled up in a jacket trying to keep warm by the fire burning low in a rusted old barrel, it was like that song from the beginning of an 80's vampire movie.

"People are strange when you're a stranger" I sang quietly as I kept my focus straight ahead.

The very thought of having to walk out of a cesspool and into something even worse was not all that appealing. I could picture all of the cunty looks I would get as I walked up the stairs to my bed. I still had the whole day before I had to go back there. I guess now I needed something to bring back to Lonzo. I found my corner, the street sign about my head letting the passing traffic know they were on Walnut Ave. This corner had been fought for buy many. In the end, Lonzo was allowed to call it his. Only his workers could hustle

8

this part of town. I needed to make some good money tonight, if I went back to the house without at least two hundred I was dead.

This fucking city was like something out of a frank miller comic book, a black and white noir with too much shadow. A loud car horn sliced through the fog. I turned to see an old station wagon, the engine sputtering, a cloud of smog following slowly behind it. The passenger side window slowly rolled down; it squeaked like it had not been used in a decade.

"What's the prices, cutie?" the man was overweight, his extra neck skin sat on his chest like a wet burrito.

"Twenty for a suck, sixty for a fuck, fifteen for a tuggy" I was able to list off prices like it was second nature, why I even mentioned the tuggy was a mystery, I had not gotten lucky enough to just do that ever.

"Seems kind of high for only two holes to choose from?" the fat trick had to catch his breath after complaining.

"Not my prices, sweetie. If you aren't interested, I need to get back to work." I tapped the hood, looking up to see if any other options were coming around. Of course I was stuck with the fat fuck, I needed to make some money.

"Well, lucky for you I just cashed my check. I have a little more to give if you don't mind going off the menu" he smiled waving his extended hand that tightly grasped a brown leather wallet.

This was not the first time I had been asked to do something that I didn't mention. It was annoying, but it was usually harmless. Some weirdo wanting me to suck his cock in front of his wife or piss on him.

"Depends on how much you're willing to spend" I said throwing him a forced smile.

"How much for you to jerk my dog off and take his load in that pretty mouth while I watch?" he asked showing a set of dark yellow teeth.

My stomach tied itself in knots, I had to let my mind process what I had just been asked.

"I'll give you a hundred and twenty" he said waving his wallet even closer to my face.

What was strange was not exactly his request, it was more the fact that the

9

super weirdos were never the first customers of the night. For as long as I could remember the nights usually started with five or six blowjobs, then maybe a couple of fucks.

A few hours into the night was when I would get the oddballs who wanted to watch me eat a corndog or take a shit in their laps. This was not a good sign being the first trick of the night but pocketing a buck twenty this early in the night would allow me to stop as early as I wanted, all while earning good for Lonzo. Maybe even take a little time before I went back to the house.

"Where's your dog?" I asked not being able to fake another smile.

The trick smiled again. I could smell his shit breath like he was inches from my face.

"Grunt!" he yelled looking in the very back.

I was startled by a large German shepherd lunging over the backseat, he landed so close that a string of his slobber smacked my lower lip. I stepped back, wiping my face with my shirt sleeve.

"Calm the fuck down goddamn it!" The trick raised his hand up, ready to back hand the dog.

"Don't hit him!" I blurted out, "Lets just go over in the alley and do this, its fine."

The trick lowed his hand, those caked over yellow teeth were in full display. I did not get in the car just yet; I showed the trick a small dark ally behind a small food mart to pull into. Grunt did cramped circles in the passenger seat, his ears standing at full attention. He was so excited just seeing someone other than the abusive dirt bag that owned him.

I walked up next to the driver's side door, the sound of rubbing metal echoed through the darkness. "Fuck." I could not help but blurt out as the trick pulled himself from the seat using the cars frame.

"If the dog and I cum, I'll definitely be a returning customer" the fat man said smiling at me from just inches away.

Now that he was out of the car I could really take in his girth. His belly hung out from the bottom of his way too small polo shirt, his jeans hanging low due to his lack of ass.

"Where do you want him?" the trick asked not taking his eyes off me.

"Um I guess the dog and I can go in the very back of the station wagon and you can watch through the window." For a moment, I thought he was going to make this even more difficult, but he nodded in approval.

As I opened the back door of the station wagon, a sickening feeling came over me. Not because of what I was about to do with a man's dog, but because something about this weirdo told me he was going to be a problem at some point during this transaction.

I need half of the payment now as insurance" I said looking over at him while Grunt, the giant German shepherd, hopped over the seat licking my face.

"Oh, sure I understand baby." The fat man opened his wallet that he still grasped firmly. He pulled out what looked like a fifty-dollar bill. "This do the trick?" he asked dangling the bill like a treat in my face.

I snatched it, crinkling it up and shoving it in my jeans pocket.

"Let me get a little more comfortable for you, baby" the fat man said, sounding like he was getting hot and bothered.

His pants hit the ground; the sound of his belt buckle made Grunt start wagging his tail in excitement. Grunt was one of the biggest dogs I had ever seen in person. His thick dark brown fur made him look even bigger, his ears still straight up, his face covered in a splash of black.

He seemed well mannered for such a large dog. I had always heard how smart German Shepard's were. I wondered how he would react to what I was about to do.

"What the fuck?" I asked looking at the fat man. He laughed while rubbing his hand where a cock should be, his fat stomach made it look like he had a pussy underneath.

I guess the fact that Grunt was trying to mount me, thrusting his hips with such force that it almost made me fall out of the car and onto the feet of the fat man.

"He's ready for you, sweetie." The fat man was sweating profusely; I could hear his teeth gritting together like rubbing stones.

11

"He's hard for you, fag boy, take him in your mouth!"

The fat fuck was breathing so heavy, I would swear that I heard his lungs deflating. Grunt's breath smelt like sardines in a hot dumpster. His paws dug into my shoulder so hard that it made my eyes tear up. I grabbed Grunt's red rocket dick and started jerking up and down on it. It was thin and wet, like sweating lipstick. As I got faster and faster, his breathing grew faster and louder. Between the mix of the fat man's body odor and grunts breath, I thought I was about to vomit.

"Oh god… oh fuck" the trick moaned and groaned. He put his hand on the roof of the car to stabilize himself, I had almost hoped he would just pass the fuck out. "Put his dick in your mouth when he starts to cum." I looked up at this fat fuck as sweat dripped from his forehead.

Suddenly a warm liquid started filling up my whitening knuckles, Grunt was Cumming like a fucking geyser.

"Fuck" I said, rolling my eyes. I leaned over and put the slimly animal cock in my mouth, the bitter warm taste of cum hit the back of my throat.

"UGH" I heard the trick moan behind me, signifying that he too just shot his load. I wanted to spit this disgusting shit out. I turned quickly before my spit mixed with the load and made my mouth fuller than what it was. I spit so fucking hard that it reminded me of a cowboy spitting his tobacco juice.

"You didn't fucking swallow?" the fat trick asked sounding angry. I looked up at his sweaty red face, his eyes looked as if the were about to explode in the sockets. "Grunt is a prized breeding dog; his fucking sperm is worth more than your miserable fucking existence!"

I had very seldomly seen someone visibly look so pissed. "I'm sorry, we never discussed the details, I figured since you had already finished it was ok" I pleaded climbing out of the car. I normally was not the type of person to plead or beg, I needed this money so badly.

"What are you going to do to make this up to Grunt and me? I am sure he's just as offended as I am." The madder this man seemed to become, the more his New York accent really showed through. I glanced over at Grunt to see him happily wagging his tail with his long pink tongue hanging from his mouth. He looked anything but offended by my actions.

"Um well I'm sorry, I really don't know what else to say. I've never done anything like this before"

I felt so pathetic trying to defend myself against this fat piece of shit. I just really wanted the money in my hand so I could get the fuck away from this fat fuck and his horny dog.

"If you want the rest of this money, you're going to get down on the ground and pick up that cum." The fat man smiled once again, flaunting his wallet in my face.

"You want me to suck it up off the ground?" I asked, disgusted. Like I had not just jerked off a dog then take his load in my mouth. Like I had standards at this point.

"Scoop it up in your thin faggy hand and stuff it in your little asshole"

I had to double take back and forth between the fat man and the puddle of cum by his feet.

"That is it? That is all I have to do for you to give me the fucking money you owe me?" I was getting a little annoyed. This is the exact reason Lonzo's henchman should be near by while we worked, it would prevent this kind of shit.

Was I about to shove this puddle of dog cum in my ass? Was this fat fuck really going to give me the money afterwards?

I wish that Ben had been my first and only customer of the night. Fuck Lonzo and his money. Instead, I was forced to humiliate myself further by doing a dance for this piece of human garbage.

"Scoop it up before it dries faggot" the fat man said with a perverse smile. I went to bend over before he stopped me, "whoa there Nancy boy, I want you to pull your pants down and then bend over and start scooping. I want to see if your wrinkled penny is pink."

I sighed looking around the dimly lit alley. I had hoped someone would drive by and maybe spook this prick into leaving. No luck. I pulled my pants down, my penis retreated into my cock sleeve from a bit of cold air hitting it.

"Grab ahold of your dick and balls while you bend over. Turn around so I can see inside you." The fat fuck was practically drooling by this point.

It always cracked me up when the more asshole tricks were closet homos who wanted to throw around words like 'faggot' and 'queer' like they were not paying a man to suck their dicks clean. They think they are showing off some kind of male dominance by cumming in a little queer's mouth or asshole. It's fucking laughable.

I squeezed tightly on what I could of my penis and slowly bent over to scrape up the dog cum with my free hand. My ass hole was spread so wide at this point I was worried the fat fuck and his horny dog would try to crawl in and stay the night.

"You keep yourself real clean, sissy" the fat man whispered in an angsty tone.

"Yeah, it is called wiping your ass. Normal people do it after they shit" I said being ass sarcastic as possible.

A hard kick in the ass crack sent me falling forward with such force that I did kind of a tumble onto the concrete. "What did you say faggot?"

I heard his voice and footsteps approaching behind me. Before I could scramble to my feet, there was another kick to knock me back down from where I started.

"I guess I don't have to worry about getting raped by a dick you can't even find" I said dazed but still aware enough to stupidly talk shit to someone kicking my ass.

"You just keep talking, don't you? How about I knock all of your fucking teeth out and make your life of dick sucking easier on the faggots that pay to fuck you."

I braced myself for the third kick, this time it caught me in between my balls and ass hole. I felt as if I was about to pass out from the lightning rod of pain that shot up through my body.

"Shut the fuck up you goddamn fucking mutt." The fat man was screaming at his dog who at this point was barking his head off.

"You're lucky I already came, or else I would fuck you dead, you little rat faggot."

I could not help but laugh on the inside. Just hearing him trying to justify himself when the truth was, he needed an atlas to find his dick.

"I'll use this instead." I slightly turned my head to look up at the fatty, he was struggling to bend over to grab an empty beer bottle that was rolling slowly between two dumpsters.

"Excuse me" a voice called out that I instantly recognized. It was the voice of my savior, the only shinning light in this shithole of a world. "Maybe you should pay the man what you owe and fuck off"

Dan stood at the end of the ally like some kind of caped superhero that heard a distress call. I could picture him jumping from the roof, landing on his feet, his hands placed firmly on his hips.

"Mind your fucking business prick, this is between me and the skinny faggot" the fat man roared. He must have been offended that he was no longer the alpha in the situation.

"Are you okay, Gavin?" Dan asked with sweet concern melting over his voice like butter on pancakes.

I nodded my head with a relieved smile.

"I said shut your fucking mouth!" the fat man screamed at Grunt, who at this point was scratching fiercely at the slightly cracked backseat window, he growled like a hungry wolf.

"Give my friend the money you owe him, then take your dog and that piece of shit car and fuck off."

The fat man became enraged. He slammed his ham-hock sized fist on the roof of the station wagon, he hit so hard that Grunt whimpered, cowering into the backseat.

"What are you going to do if I don't, faggot lover?" the fat man asked taking a few steps towards dans silhouette.

Dan pulled back the side of his tan trench coat, the dim alley light reflected off the chrome handgun tucked nicely in a brown leather holster on his hip.

"You a cop?" the fat man asked. taking back the few steps he already taken.

"I could be. You want to find out, fatty? Give the man his money and leave."

The fat man stood there for a moment trying to decide if he wanted to take the risk. "Fuck you and this sickly-looking queer. Have fun popping the blister on your lip afterwards" the fat man said making one last comment before throwing a wad of cash on the ground next to where I laid.

He climbed in the front seat, the car screeched and moaned as if it was in pain. Before I knew it, there was a cloud of exhaust in my face as the old station wagon roared out of sight. I looked up through the smog to see my big dick in shining armor, extending his hand to help me up.

CHAPTER 2: THE SPANIARD

"Saying that I'm glad to see you would be the understatement of the century" I said awkwardly pulling my pants up.

Dan was about six-three or four, burly, trimmed five o'clock shadow, a head of coal black hair slicked back like superman.

"I was on patrol over on Honeysuckle. Got a call about a disturbance over this way. I figured it was you or one of your acquaintances working the alley."

He kept looking around, kind of like someone who visits your house for the first time and are constantly looking around. You start to feel that overwhelming paranoia that they are secretly judging your choice of furniture, the color of the walls, or the pizza box left on the kitchen table.

"Well good thing you stopped by. I would have limped home broke, with a beer bottle in my ass." I laughed only for Dan to shake his head and smile, he was such a stern man, chiseled from granite.

I knew he was married by the tan line on his left ring finger, either he took of the ring for work, or he took it off for play. Either way, Dan was in the closet.

"Haven't you ever considered a safer line of work?" he asked, flicking a match on the brick wall beside us, the flame lit up his face as he sucked in on a lit hand rolled cigarette.

"I could ask you the same question?" I said with a smile as I took another micro step closer to him.

The cigarette smoke made my eyes burn and my mouth water, no one ever made smoking a coffin nail look so goddamn good. Dan leaned against the wall, taking his cigarette out to blow a cloud of smoke into the night sky.

"This job is all I've ever known. Been at it since I was twenty. I've learned these streets above and below. I've been pushed and tested beyond my limits, but still, I wake up every morning and do the same shit over and over."

He was staring a hole through the dumpster on the other side of the alley. I could see the wheels turning in his head. I was his street therapist. I was the one who listened to him when he wanted to get that dark shit off his chest that he could not go home and tell his wife. I was his shameful secret kept locked away from the rest of his world. Honestly, I didn't mind a bit.

"Well, it's good to see you. I wish it had been under better circumstances, but you get what you get" I said, wishing he would just look at me for even a second. "You want me to suck your dick? It is on the house?" I said trying not to sound sad and desperate for his attention.

He stared a few seconds longer at the dumpster before throwing the finished cigarette but on the ground, smushing it with the heal of his dress shoe.

"I'm not sure if I have time to night, I might have to take you up on that some other night" he turned slightly, giving me a reassuring wink.

What did he think this was? I only offered because I liked him and have enough money now to fuck around. My nights were not usually taken so easily.

"Well, ok" I said crossing my arms like a pouty little bitch. He must have noticed because I felt his arm wrap around my waist, the hairs on my neck stood up.

"How bad do you want to suck this cock?" he whispered in my ear; the smell of smoke still hot on his breath.

I turned to look him in the face, I tried to play it cool but inside I was jumping up and down. "I guess I can fit you into my busy schedule."

I smiled puckering my lips and tilting my head, did I have to come off like such a fag? In retrospect it was astonishing that I even found myself in the mood for any form of sexual activity.

"Meet me at the Days inn over off Jericho in about an hour?" he asked, but it didn't sound much like a question. He knew I wasn't turning down a hotel room. In this line of work, outsiders always assume that we're always meeting clients in seedy motels off the highway. In reality, you were lucky to get a trick to take you anywhere other than their backseat. A few hours in a room with a bed and a tv was a rare luxury in my line of work, a luxury that Dan was always willing to share with me.

"I'll be there" I said with another wink. Was I winking too much? Fuck... probably.

"I'll keep an eye out the window. Maybe we'll get lucky and end up in room number nine like last time" he said rubbing my arm with the back of his hand.

Cold chills covered my body like a bad case of poison ivy. "That would be pretty nice" I said trying to keep from winking again, he thought I was fucking retarded.

As Dan turned and walked away down the alley, a flood of negative thoughts started trying to bury this happy moment under a ton of dirt.

He's married, he doesn't give a damn about you. You're just a suck hole for his cock. After he cums, he'll toss a few dollars at your feet as he pulls his pants up.

I shook my head, trying to just enjoy the moment. These thoughts had haunted me for as long as I could remember. Anything positive, be it minor or significant, was eaten alive by all the things that could go wrong... That, or it was my brain actually trying to convince my emotions to be logical.

I mean, did I really expect Dan to just throw his life away for some skinny street queer who sucked a good dick? Was he going to take me to the policeman's ball and flaunt me to all his equally closeted male co-workers?

No... That was purely a fantasy and nothing more. In the time waiting to meet up with Dan, I made a few more dollars letting some old guy play with my ass hole while he told me stories of the fifties. It was clear that he was not able to get hard anymore. Making money just to have your pants down, bent over the hood of a blue ford pick-up while your shit-slit was fingered by the crypt keepers' hands was not a bad night's work.

Stuffing the wad of crinkled bills into my front pocket made the imagine of Lonzo appear, ready to defile even my smallest semblance of joy. "Better get me my money, fuck boy!"

I could smell his breath even in my imagination. I rubbed my eyes while trying to pick up the broken shards of glass that was once the window to my sanity.

"Come away with me, lets leave tonight and go anywhere you want baby."

I closed my eyes to picture Dan sitting naked on the hotel sheets begging me to just get the fuck out of this shit hole city with him. Italy, France, the Virgin Islands, anywhere I wanted to go. I shook my head and took a deep breath. I had a better chance of my long dead father apologizing for mouth-fucking me when I was ten... it was a nice thought though. As I walked down the sidewalk, my shadow raced in front of me like it was excited to see Dan.

"Go home, bitch!" a group of what looked to be teenagers shouted from the opposite side of the road.

"Hey, I got a quarter if you'll eat my friend's ass hole!" They laughed like a rabid group of hyenas. I ignored them and kept walking.

I could feel the wad of money in my pocket. To most, it would be a sense of accomplishment. To me, it was a ticket to keep all my teeth.

"Keep walking you pink haired queer!" The kids were still laughing, punching each other in the arms. Trying to stay cool in their small social circle.

I laughed to myself thinking about how high the chances were that one of their dads had his dick in my ass or mouth. The vacancy light above the hotel flickered like a nightclub strobe light. My heart raced from the overwhelming excitement.

I stood for a few moments, staring up at the white door with a gold painted '9'. I pictured Dan sitting on the bed with his thick cock wrapped tightly in his hand, just getting harder and harder thinking about it going deeper and deeper down my throat. The stairs lasted an eternity before I reached the door. I had no clue if he was even able to get this room. Even with the blinds drawn shut, I could see the light coming from the small lamp by the bed.

20

"Dan?" I asked, just loud enough in the hopes that the blinds in the neighboring rooms did not start popping open. The eyes of wondering strangers looking out at a pink haired twink.

I was startled by the door latch unlocking. The butterflies in my stomach were the size of fruit bats. I felt like a boy asking out his first high school girlfriend. Why I was so nervous was difficult to explain. I had been here with Dan before; this was not anything new. It was the fact that I really felt something for Dan, something I have never felt for anyone.

"Can I help you?" a Hispanic looking man asked, poking his head out the door.

"Oh, I'm sorry I must have the wrong room. I was looking for a friend that I thought was staying here." I could feel my face grow red from the embarrassment. What if Dan was watching me from another room? Laughing his ass off at my expense.

"What's the name of this friend, if you don't mind me asking?" the man asked, scratching at his chin. A thick black mustache covered his top lip.

"Um, well I'm not sure I should say. It's kind of a personal thing."

What if this man was Dan's partner on the police force? What if this guy knew Dan in any capacity?

"You look familiar, have we meet somewhere before?" The man stepped out of the dimly lit room. He looked to be in his late twenties or early thirties. His haircut looked like a military fade, his eyes dark and piercing.

"Oh, so like a secret agent meeting? You an undercover agent guy?" the man asked with a hint of a Spanish accent.

"Um, no. I'm just meeting a friend." I was really regretting not just waiting until Dan came out of which ever room he was in and just wave me over.

This guy was super strange. I had met some weird people in my line of work, some of them could be a little intense to say the least. Something about this guy was on another level.

"Well, if you tell me this 'friends' name, I might be able to help you. That way you do not have to come whispering in people's windows like some fucking gay prowler." He smiled at his little jab. He was definitely enjoying this way too much.

"Sorry to disturb you, goodnight." I rolled my eyes as I started to walk towards the steps.

"You walk away like? Like some little bratty bitch who likes to roll their eyes? I guess you will not be seeing Dan tonight." I stopped dead in my tracks. How did he know I was meeting with dan? Was this fucked up joke?

"How do you know Dan? Better question is how did you know that I was meeting him?" I asked trying to keep my temper in check.

"Whoa there, pink panther. Let some air out of that flat chest and calm down. I am an old friend of Dan's. I stopped by to visit him. He told me he was having some 'off the books company' coming over, so I assume that's you… Right?" his raised one eyebrow with his arms crossed.

Dan told someone about us? He called it 'off the books company'? I mean, I know that we're not a couple or anything, but 'off the books company' seemed so… I could not think of the word for it, I just knew that it was not like Dan to just go around telling people about these secret rendezvous.

"Is Dan inside?" I asked trying to peak around the man to see in the room.

"Yeah, he's here. His heads in the toilet, must have eaten something that didn't sit well. Come on in and you can wait for him on the bed"

The man stepped aside to let me through. Something was seriously wrong here. Was this some kind of sting operation where I was going to be thrown on the floor and arrested by a swat team? I had been arrested a handful of times since I started working the streets. I never did any hard time, just a few overnighters.

Jail was not the worst place in the world compared to Lonzo's castle of Gays. At least in jail, when someone does not like you, they aren't afraid to come right out and say it. Plus, surviving would not be as hard for myself as it would be for some skinny straight white man who is never sucked a dick.

"Have a seat on the bed and I'll see if our buddy Dan is feeling better."

The strange Spanish man walked over towards the bathroom door, his hands were buried in the pockets of his faded denim jacket, his jeans tucked lazily into a polished pair of brown leather cowboy boots.

"Dan, you have a visitor."

I sat, watching who I would refer to at this point as the Spaniard, knock softly on the door with the back of his pointer and index finger. Did Dan plan this? Was this his way of roping me in to a three-some? Whatever it was, I was not a fan.

"Dan, buddy. You still alive in there? Ready or not, I am coming in." The Spaniard turned and flashed a quick smile at me before opening the door and quickly disappearing into the small bathroom.

I tried to listen to see if I could hear Dans voice, at least some sign that he was here.

"Your face is still buried in that toilet? What am I supposed to do with your skinny little friend out there?" was all I could hear before the sound of a running faucet muffled the Spaniard's voice. After a few moments the bathroom door opened, my heart raced hoping to see Dan all better with a smile on his face just for me.

"He's still not doing too well buddy, but he said you're more than welcome to come in and see him" the Spaniard whispered as he walked over towards the bed.

"Did he ask for me?" I asked curiously.

The Spaniard popped down on the other bed, putting his hands behind his head, he took a deep breath than looked over at me for a few seconds before smiling at me again.

"I told him you were here. He did not exactly say to let you in, but I think he could use some comfort in the state he is in right now."

I looked at the Spaniard, and then over at the bathroom door. "Do you work with Dan?" I asked looking back over at the Spaniard who was now kicking off his cowboy boots and stretching out.

"Dan and I met through a mutual friend. Basically, I was the guy who came home from work one day and caught some guy fucking my wife in the ass over our island countertop." I was surprised by the Spaniards answer, obviously.

"Yeah. He pulled his shit covered dick out of her ass to explain that he had no idea that she was married, started begging and pleading for me to forget the whole thing. Said he was married, and his wife would kill him if she found out."

I sat there listening, wondering if Dan was hearing this same story from the other side of the bathroom wall. I never really thought much about the time that Dan and I were not together physically. His personal life was a mystery that I did not care much about solving.

"So, the two of you are friends now after something like that?" I asked with a knot forming in my gut. The Spaniard just stared off into space like he was replaying the scene in his mind.

"My wife was going to leave me for some burnt out piece of shit cop who had a son that didn't give a fuck about him, and two failed marriages. What the fuck did she see in this motherfucker?" His fist started clenching loud enough that I could hear his knuckles pop.

"Who the fuck did that bitch think that she was?" he stood up and started pacing back and forth. His use of past tense made that knot grow exponentially in size. Something was horribly wrong here.

"Is Dan dead in that bathroom?" That was the only thing I could muster up, the only thing I cared about in the world.

A relieved sigh from the Spaniard answered my question. The room started spinning around the killers twisted smile. I was the punch line in a twisted joke, or player one in a game created by a psychopath. My hands pushed my body up off the bed, my legs carried me unwillingly to the bathroom door. The Spaniard did not seem to care what I would see at this point.

I knew that seeing Dan dead would ultimately be the thing that killed me. Not from the horrible sight of his mangled body, but the Spaniard that undoubtably would leave no witness. The bathroom door was cheap, thin, and familiar.I had been in it before. I had pissed in its toilet; I had washed off in its shower.

My mind had always been a cruel and unforgiving bully, it forced my body to experience things that not many people could even comprehend. The thick smell of copper filled the small room, the wallpaper that had once depicted little sailboats now soaked up dark red blood like an old sponge. The door flexed near the bottom, the weight of a headless body wearing a tan trench coat nudged slightly on the sticky blood covered floor. My eyes were forced to dart from top to bottom of the room, only to see the wet, matted, once perfectly combed hair sticking slightly above the rim of the now red painted toilet.

"Dan...no...please!" My words shook at the same speed as my quivering hands. A step forward created a loud scratching metallic sound, a large fire axe wobbled for a moment before coming to a dead stop.

"Were you his sweet pink cupcake?" a voice behind me whispered next to my earlobe. If I had been naked, I would have been mistaken for a sickly skinny version of the statue of David, liquid concrete replaced the blood that kept me alive.

"Personally, I doubt he loved you. I think he was simply an ass man. You and my wife were the shit dick he wasn't allowed at home." The Spaniard's breath was warm on the back of my neck now.

I opened my mouth to speak, but it was like being trapped in a nightmare where everything was in slow motion, I screamed but deafening silence wrapped its hands tight around my throat. A sharp pain in the back of my head violently flicked off the light switch to my consciousness.

CHAPTER 3: THIS HOUSE SUCKS

"If I have to tell you to get up again, I'll drag you the fuck out of that bed by your fucking hair!" my mom screamed. My eyes shot open as the sun hit my face through the smudged window in my bedroom.

"What are you screaming about now bitch?" my dad's voice followed.

"That fucking worthless excuse for a son of yours has been told twice now to get out of bed. Maybe you need to try" before my mom put the period on her response, I was up and out of bed so fast that it made the room spin. Footsteps thudding down the short hallway made my body tense up; I was in for it now.

"Do your fucking ears need to be checked, retard?" my father asked sticking his head around the door frame. His beard had grown thick while the hair on his head had grown thin, his blue eyes deeper than any ocean.

"No sir, I was just getting dressed." He looked my up and down. I had hoped to be wearing more than a pair of briefs before he came stopping down the hall. My bad luck was not changing today.

"Did you wear those exact same underwear yesterday?" he asked as his eyes still slowly made their way up and down my slender boyish frame. I tried to open my mouth, but the cottonmouth had sewn it shut, I just nodded.

"Well, you're not going to wear them again today, are you boy?" His words sent a trail of acid down my windpipe. "Your dumbass mother isn't worth much, but she sure knows how to do your fucking laundry. Put on a clean pair. Hand me those and I'll toss them in the hamper for you."

His bad breath filled the small bedroom faster the heavier he would breathe.

"Come on, goddamn it. I don't have all goddamn day to wait on some sissy ass queer to pull off his little panties."

My mother walked past behind my father holding my two-year-old baby brother Keith, he smiled when we made eye contact. "You finally got him out of bed, I see" my mom said slowly bouncing Keith on her hip.

"Take your ass in the bathroom and clean up the fucking mess you made earlier" my dad said, slightly turning to stare down my mother. She looked up at him for a moment before glancing over at me.

"You must be as deaf as your faggot son!" he yelled so loud that the walls of the tiny trailer shook. Keith let out a high-pitched cry that could shatter glass. My mother pulled him close to her chest in an attempt at comforting him.

"If you don't walk in the other room and shut that fucking baby up, I swear I'll smash both of your fucking skulls in."

My mother turned and quickly made her way out of sight, hushing Keith on the way.

"Don't threaten my brother like that again you fat fucking prick piece of shit!" My fathers eyes grew so large it looked like they were having trouble staying in the sockets. I had never in my life stood up to my him, never had I spoken back, never had I raised my voice in his direction.

My father was a piece of fucking shit. My mother spent all her time kissing his ass making sure he was happy, even resorting to calling me a faggot to make him laugh. Keith, on the other hand was innocent and unaffected by their cruelty, unless he turns out to be a fifteen-year-old who gets caught with a queer porno magazine under his bed. I was not going to stand by while this fat prick threatened the only good thing about this family.

"What the fuck did you just say to me you little dick sucking freak?" My father stepped forward, he reached down and picked up a studded belt I had secretly made in shop class. "You like wearing nail polish and faggoty shit like this? You think cause you are some fucking pole smoker that I won't beat your fucking brains in?"

My father slung the belt like a whip across the room, the end hit me in my right eye, colorful spots blind me for a moment. "All my fucking friends laughing about my son, the faggot. How fucking embarrassing do you think that is?" I could hear his voice, but my sight still had not come back, which would have help me prepare for the next smack with the belt that caught me across the side of the thigh.

"Stop!" I screamed in pain. At this point in my life I almost had to fake the pain, after so long it becomes routine.

"You still want to suck dick boy?!" he shouted in my face; the belt was wrapped tightly around his fist.

"I'm sorry!" I screamed shielding my face the best I could.

"Get on your knees!" a hard punch to the gut made it impossible to not fall straight to my knees, gasping for breath.

"Please, don't dad." It hurt to even speak; my stomach ached as If I had been struck by lightning. I saw his pants drop to the ground around his ankles in front of me.

"You'll suck my cock now, or I'll go rip that future faggot from your dumbass mom and make him suck it." His words hurt more than his punch. "Come on, a dick is a dick, and you like them all. If you're going to be a cocksucker you better get to practicing"

I leaned my head up to see my father holding his penis just inches from my face. "I woke your mother up with a good ass fucking this morning. I haven't washed her stink off yet."

I fought to swallow the vomit that filled my mouth.

* * *

"Wake up baby, you don't want to miss this" a man's voice that was not my fathers called out close enough to my face that I could smell the cheese omelet he had for breakfast.

"Look at what I did for you." The voice belonged to the Spaniard.

He knelt in front of me as the world came back in focus. The first thing I noticed immediately was that my mouth was stuffed with what felt like an

28

old dirty washrag. The second was the odd sensation of sharp prickles all over my body, like I had fallen in a thorn bush.

"I didn't think you were ever going to wake up, pinky man" the Spaniard said, smiling as he sat Indian style just a few feet from me. It did not take much longer to realize that my upper body was bound tightly in barbed-wire so silver that if you were to squint closely you would almost see your reflection.

"You like that? I had that shit specially made for your friend in the bathroom, but I let my feelings get the best of me and forgot to use it."

He observed his handy work like it was a piece of barbaric artwork. I tried to sit to the side, but instantly, the barbs dug deeper into my bare arms.

"Whoa there, pretty in pink. I don't want you bleeding out so quickly, I want you to enjoy this for as long as you can." He smiled as he stood up and patted me on the head.

I was sitting in the far corner of the room. The lights were dimmer than they were before, the bathroom door still open wide enough to make out the chunks of flesh that rested in the sporadic puddles of blood.

"Now, you must have some questions, like 'why are you doing this to me? Why don't you just kill me and get it over with?' But, all that will be obvious in due time." He sat there so proud of himself. I did not need any questions answered. I knew why he was doing this and why he did not just get it over with.

"Just know that I'm not the bad guy here. That piece of shit in the bathroom is the one who came into my home and butt-fucked his way into this situation!" The Spaniard was becoming visibly angry.

The thought of Dan bending his wife over and fucking her hard enough to make her tits bounce out of her bra oddly made me smile on the inside.

"This is just one of those, how do you say 'right place, wrong time' situations."

The Spaniard walked over to a black trash bag that set like a clump of coal in the corner by the bed table. "I do not think you deserve to be tortured. I do not think you are even a bad guy like your boyfriend. I don't even care that you are gay. I am going to torture you because the man that ruined my life enjoyed the pleasure of your company." He sighed and reached deep into the black trash bag. "I know that sounds like a very stupid reason to go to these lengths, but ever since I stuck my wife in a wooden crate and buried her alive under our basement floor, I've had this new drive."

He smiled at me as he pulled what looked to be a red and black cordless power drill for the crinkled black bag. My eyes grew large, my skin went a shade whiter than it already was, my heart pounded. "Do you like this pinky boy?"

He held it up in the air as he pulled the small black trigger; the little motor grinded loudly, the serrated blade he had crudely fashioned to the end spun to fast for my eyes to keep up. The room started to get fuzzy. I could feel a bead of sweat race down my forehead and into my brow.

"Fu-" I tried to scream out for help but the rag was shoved so far in my mouth that I could not even wiggle my tongue.

"Now look, I am sensitive to your lifestyle. I know that you spend a lot of time with things up your rear… so I'm going to give you a break, because as I said before, I am not that bad guy."

I didn't understand where in the hell he was going with this. I mean, my first thought was that he was going to just drill into me until I bled out all over the place, not that he was going to go straight for my ass hole.

"I am going to do something I bet none of your clients would even consider. I'm going to give your dick some serious attention." He smiled as he revved the drill back up.

My heart ripped through my chest and caught the next flight to Alaska.

"Do you think this blade will shred your dick within seconds? Or spin for a bit if I try to keep my hand steady?" He looked down at me with what seemed like legitimate professional curiosity. "I would take out your gag to hear what you think, but I can't afford to having you screaming loud enough to wake the other nice people staying here." He smiled at me like I was a child he refused giving a cookie to before dinner.

"Let's take a look what we have in here." He sat the drill to the side as he knelt next to me. He pushed his sunglasses back up with his pointer finger.

30

"Damn things cost me a fortune, but will never stay in place."

He shook his head and laughed. When he finally had my dick in his hand he looked up and smiled at me. I assumed his teeth were perfect for a Spanish psychopath, but I was not an expert in the matter. Once my limp cock was squeezed tightly in his grip, I thought about what the aftermath of this torture would be like. A dickless male prostitute, a transvestite street walker, a cockless pink haired queer.

But, I guess it would not be all bad. The Spaniard was right about one thing... My dick never really received the attention anyway. I was either taking it in the ass or taking a hot load in the mouth. It's not like anyone ever paid to suck me off.

"I hope that we can be friends afterwards, pink boy" the Spaniard said, still holding that same smile.

"I'm sure you'll be invited over to the house of twinks for a Thanksgiving dinner." I would have said if I could speak.

"Will you not think of me as some kind of perverted monster? This is not personal, my friend" he assured me as the smile turned upside down with an intense seriousness. This guy was truly fucking nuts. I mean, I knew he was crazy after seeing how he decorates motel bathrooms, but this... this begging of me to not take mutilating my genitals seriously? Fuck.

"This is the one, baby" a third voice came into this macabre scene. The Spaniard and I both looked over in surprise, a muscular black man and a short stubby little balding guy walked right through the unlocked room door. Needless to say, they were a lot more surprised at what they were seeing compared to the Spaniard and I.

"Gavin?" the muscular black guy asked staring at me in shock.

Fuck, I knew he looked somewhat familiar. He used to live in Lonzo's house with myself and a few others, I hadn't seen him in over a year or so.

"Is this part of the surprise?" the fat stumpy bald man asked with a curious smile.

"I don't know what the fuck this shit is?" the black man said with one

31

eyebrow raised high.

"Please excuse us gentleman. We are just in the middle of some foreplay. I would really like to get back to what I paid my hard-earned money for" the Spaniard said as he stood and bowed gracefully.

For the life of me I could not remember the black man's name, Tyrell? Tye something? Fuck, I could not remember, but I was not going to let him just walk back out that door thinking this was some kind of fucked up roleplay. I started shaking my head and making as many distressed sounds as I could. Tyrell looked down at me, Tyrell? Tyler? Taebo? I did not fucking know. Right now, he was Tyrell, and he was my only hope of leaving here with a fully functional penis.

"Take that gag out of his mouth so I can hear what he has to say" Tyrell ordered the Spaniard.

"My good sir, I am a paying customer and I want what I paid for. You and your friend here are ruining this experience for me" the Spaniard said in a play-acting kind of voice.

Tyrell did not look convinced; his eyebrow was still high up on his forehead as he looked down at me and then back up at the Spaniard.

"Take the fucking gag out, or I'll beat your weird little ass and do it myself" Tyrell demanded as he pointed his huge pointer finger down at me. Tyrell looked like one of those bodybuilders you see working out by the beach in Florida, thigh high shorts and a tank-top that was hardly a shirt anymore. The Spaniard grew quiet as he stared intensely through his aviators at Tyrell.

"This man's closet gay lover fucked my wife in the ass. I cut his head off with a fire axe I found in a case on the wall outside the room" the Spaniard proclaimed with his arms crossed. The room was silent for a few moments, even Tyrell's customer looked taken aback by what the Spaniard claimed.

"You did what?" Tyrell asked like he had suddenly lost that boom in his voice.

"You heard me you big dumb monkey. I decapitated Pinky's boyfriend in the bathroom with a goddamn fire axe. Now if you will please excuse us, I am going to shove this homemade drill-tip up Pinky's cock hole. I promise there is no intention to kill him. I only wish to maim him." The Spaniard must have felt as if this were a minor inconvenience for him. Like these onlookers would just pass and allow him to finish what he had planned.

"Go down to the payphone and call the police" Tyrell demanded his customer with the boom back in his voice. The little bald man looked at Tyrell, the Spaniard, and then me.

"I um... do not want to be involved in this. Can't we just find the right room and do what I am paying you to do? I must get home soon" the man whined like a small child wanting candy in the checkout line.

"Go call the fucking police, Mickey!" Tyrell shouted so loudly that I think even the Spaniard may have pissed himself.

"Son of a bitch" the Spaniard grunted as he grew irritated. A loud pop that sounded like a firecracker going off in an empty soda can made my ears ring. When it happened, I was staring at fat Mickey, hoping he would shut the fuck up and call the police. Then, in the blink of an eye, the back of his head exploded on the wall behind him.

"What the fuck!?" screamed Tyrell as he lunged forward like a linebacker, knocking the shiny pistol from the Spaniard's extended arm.

They both hit the floor with a thud, the gun flew across the room smacking the bathroom door. I tried to roll, but the barbed wire dug deeper and deeper with every failed attempt. Tyrell and the Spaniard wrestled violently on the floor in front of the bed, it was shocking to see the Spaniard put up such a fight with Tyrell being twice his size.

"Mother fucker!" Tyrell screamed in pain as the Spaniard shoved a thumb in Tyrells left eye.

I had to do something. I rolled to my side, the barbed wire sliced and poked without remorse. A barb getting caught on the carpet allowed me to unwind myself from its clutches. Blood trickled down both of my arms, my shirt began sticking to my chest and back. I imagined it was not sweat gluing it to me. I looked up in time to see the Spaniard reach the gun that still rested peacefully in front of the bathroom/crypt where it had landed. Luckily, Tyrell made it to his feet before the Spaniard could once again extend his arm to fire. A shot went off towards the ceiling, it snowed drywall.

Tyrell slung the Spaniard with all his might sending him soaring through the air and crashing into the small entertainment center ."Don't move, you sick fuck!" Tyrell now had his massive arm extended; in his hand the shiny pistol was his sword of justice.

"So, what do you plan on doing with that, ape man?" the Spaniard asked as he pulled himself back to his feet, his nose and lip still bloody from the battle.

"Gavin, get up and use the room phone to call the front desk. Tell them to call the police" Tyrell demanded without taking his eyes off the Spaniard.

I pulled the dirty rag from my mouth, finally being able to breathe properly. "Thank you for this. Thank you for saving my life" I said panting.

"No time for that. Get on the phone" Tyrell's left eye was swollen and bloody, it was hard to tell if there was even still an eye there.

"I will not be going to jail tonight" the Spaniard said smiling. The blood ran down into his mouth, staining his teeth. "I will kill both of you mother fuckers. The maid will be cleaning your fucking teeth up from the carpet when I've finished with you!"

Tyrell did not respond with words to the Spaniards threats, he just took a step forward and smacked the Spaniard across the face with the pistol. The sound of metal against flesh was so pleasant in this instance.

"I know this is an awkward time to ask... is your name Tyrell?" Tyrell turned and looked at me for the first time since the fight began.

"You really don't remember my goddamn name, Gavin?" he asked, offended. I stood there for a moment hoping it would come to me so we could move past this, but my mind drew a blank once more.

"My fucking name is Gregory. How the fuck are you going to forget a black man named Gregory? I mean goddamn, Gavin. We lived together in that nasty ass cum house together long enough for you to at least learn my mutha fucking name." This man had just risked his life to save mine, and I couldn't even remember the whitest name in the history of names.

34

"Sorry about that. I guess a lot has been going on since you left the house" I said with a shrug.

"Cock sucker!" the Spaniard screamed out. He tackled into Gregory, knocking him onto the bed. "I'll kill you and that little mother fucker!"

I did not see the gun in Gregory's hand anymore. He must have dropped it in the struggle. The Spaniard paid me no mind as he started punching Gregory in the head with vicious blows. He hit him at least ten times before I noticed the power drill still sitting on the floor, the same power drill that almost made me lose the one attractive head I had on my body.

"Choke, monkey!" the Spaniard screamed as he wrapped his hands around Gregory's massive neck.

Blue and red lights came through the window, lighting the room up like a rave party. Someone must have called them because of the gunshots, which was surprising in this neighborhood. The Spaniard did not take his eyes off of Gregory, who he was still choking the life out of.

I did the only thing I could think to do, I picked up the drill and with everything I had to give. I stuck the tip of it right into the side of the Spaniards face.

"Fuck!" the Spaniard cried out in agony. Before he could pull away, I squeezed down on the trigger, the homemade blade started spinning as the motor revved up to full speed. Blood and spit shot out like putting two tomatoes in a blender without putting the lid on properly. For a moment before he flung himself backwards, I could feel the drill blade dig into his teeth.

"On the fucking ground!" was the first thing I heard when the motel door was kicked to splinters.

"Get on the ground goddamn it!" Two black machine guns pointed directly in my face.

CHAPTER 4: NOBODY

A month had passed by since that night in the motel room. A month had passed since I was hammed for nine straight hours in a small windowless room about what happened.

I had not heard anything about Gregory or the Spaniard. I assume the Spaniard was either dead or in critical condition someplace far away. Dan's wife didn't believe any of what I had to say. She called me a weird fucking freak that had a creepy 'gay obsession' with her perfect husband. The police completely discredited me as well, they knew it was true, but they certainly weren't about to let it out that one of their detectives was out fucking male prostitutes and fucking random housewives in the ass. I was let go when they found the body of Mrs. Shelly Hernandez in a box, buried alive in the cement floor of her and Mr. Pedro Hernandez's basement. When I read about it in the paper, there was no mention of mine nor Gregory's name, only that a decorated police detective was murdered by some Spanish immigrant wife killer. I was a nobody once more, forgotten and thrown to the side, it was better this way.

I sat up from the hard floor, the sleeping bag I had been sleeping in for the past few weeks was now used strictly as a blanket.

"Another day of sucking dick awaits us, fellas" a voice from the bed I was partially under sung out. "Everyone make sure you wash up and give it your all out there today. Lonzo has given us a place to sleep, food, and money in our pockets. Let's not disappoint him."

I rolled my eyes in disgust, what a fucking kiss ass Nicholas was. Nicholas was Lonzo's second favorite out of this band of queer trash. Behind his back, he was called Lonzo's personal little Nazi. Nicholas, like a few others, was allowed to have the beds. Not like they were fancy beds, bunk beds cut down into separates. If you were a top earner or royal ass kisser, you were blessed with a decent night sleep and a better cut of your earnings. I could make sixty dollars and be left with ten if Lonzo was in a good mood.

The house was run down so badly that I am surprised it did not have a condemned sticker pasted to the front door like an eviction notice. If it had, Lonzo probably greased the right set of hands to be allowed to keep and operate out of it. I am sure at one point the wallpaper was not peeling away like skin after a bad sunburn. I'm sure the carpets in each room once had a certain plush to them, but now they were matted to the floor like old wet newspaper.

"Would you just shut the fuck up Nicholas? Not all of us are so eager to go out and suck dick for pennies" the gayest sounding whore in the room spoke up.

"You shut the fuck up, Adam. You're just jealous that I'm one of Lonzo's favorites. That's why I make good money and sleep in a bed. That's why you are down there on the floor with the rest of the garbage. Why Lonzo keeps any of you around is beyond my comprehension."

Adam stuck his tongue out and rolled his eyes at the overly bitchy twink prince.

Nicholas did not look like the average queer; he was heavier set with the slightest hint of a double chin starting to peak its way out like a baby kangaroo in its mother's pouch. He had a baby face with big innocent eyes, though if you knew anything about Nicholas, you knew damn well there was nothing innocent about him. I am sure once he got up to get dressed, he would put on the tightest clothes he could find. Just enough for his belly to hang out. He said that his cuteness and weight went together like cum and donuts. I never understood how the two went together at all.

The one upside to this shit nest that benefitted Nicholas and his fat rolls was the beef stew and potatoes that we were served twice a week. Other than that, we had to fend for ourselves. Then there was Adam, Jeremy, Jordan, and Gilly. Gilly was one of the few people in the house that I could hold a conversation with, even though it was always gossip and drama.

"Did you hear that the new guy sucks at giving head?" I remember him coming to me smiling while I waited outside the downstairs bathroom door.

"Yeah, Lonzo had one of his henchmen knock some of his teeth out because he overly used them."

He would snicker and walk away to gossip to someone else. He was slightly taller than me with a faded hair cut that made him look like he was a member of Hitlers youth group. I felt as if I were trapped in a never ending hell with a bunch of gay demons that would screech and claw at one another over a quarter found lodged in the couch cushion.

"Creepy Kenny" I heard someone snicker as I dug through my trash bag of clothes that I kept stored on the closet shelf, right next to the jugs of lube and unopened boxes of cheap condoms.

"Creepy Kenny." I heard again. Without having to turn around I knew what the joke was and at whom it was directed.

"Shut the fuck up with that shit, you scrawny bitch!" a raspy voice belonging to the aforementioned Kenny. "I'm sick of you gay boy fucks always running your painted on cocksuckers!"

Kenny had just walked in and was immediately the ass end of a joke that he did not understand. Kenny was the straightest looking gay guy that I had ever seen. I mean, he was either just playing gay for the money , which looking straight earned him a lot, or he could be gayer than a case of aids. Kenny had a military type of hair cut with a very superhero jawline; he was also in tremendous physical shape.

"Come on, creepy Kenny. You know we're just messing with you." Nicholas laughed as he pulled the tiny polo over his huge bitch tits.

"Well, you seem to be the only person making jokes around this fucking house" Kenny said angrily pointing his finger in Nicholas's direction.

I had heard the rumors about Kenny, straight from Gilly, the gay whisperer. Kenny was the brother on one of the henchmen that followed Lonzo around. I was not sure if it was the one who sucked his cock, or wiped his asshole after a shit. Gilly would say that Kenny was not always gay, that he had beaten his girlfriend to death with a sledgehammer one night while she was sleeping comfortably in bed. I asked Gilly why, and after looking around for a second to make sure no one else heard his big mouth, he said that she had caught him beating off to a queer magazine. She said it was ok and that she would forget the whole thing, but he did not believe her.

Gilly claimed that he heard Kenny had hit her in the face once and while she was barely hanging on, he hit he between the legs with the hammer, causing her to die from the pain.

"Lonzo had his guys rape her dead body afterwards in some alley way. Told Kenny he had to come work for him to pay off the debt" he whispered. I took everything that Gilly said with a grain of salt and a shot of penicillin. In this house, gossip was the only form of entertainment.

"The tricks are going to love it." I heard Jordan squeal as I came out of my trance. He held up this ugly ass lime green fish net tank top. I was not really one for fashion, so what would I know on the subject? It did not take Tommy Hilfiger to determine that these types of gays weren't the fun dressing up high school best friend that every girl friend-zoned. These were the mean, nasty, spiteful gays. The scum that even the cheapest female street walker looked down upon. I was no exception, I was no better than this group of dick bitches. Only. in my opinion. I was lightyears smarter. A faded black Tool shirt and a pair of baggy jeans was my outfit of choice. I really did not have a character like the others, they all put their clothes and makeup on like they were preforming on broadway.

"Any of you bitches seen my fucking blueberry bomb lipstick? That shit was expensive" Either I couldn't tell who asked, or I didn't care.

"Listen up cunts!" a dreadfully familiar voice called from the hallway outside the door. Lonzo entered the room in some kind of red velvet smokers' jacket, his frizzy ass hair put up in a bun.

"Are you worthless fucks going to go out there and make me some money tonight, come home and sleep under my roof? Or are you going to be another homeless faggot, begging for money?"

I could not help but shake my head, he played these people like they were nothing before him. Truth is, we were nothing before Lonzo. Now, we were all just nothings living under the same roof. This humanitarian of the year graced the trash he saved from the street with one bedroom to share between seven. Meanwhile, Lonzo slept upstairs in a newly renovated section of this dump that a rat would not even shit on. Those of us who were fortunate enough to have seen upstairs made the envy for this low-life pimp grow at an alarming rate. It was sad, really, to have nothing but a sawed-off closeted dick sucking 2-bit pimp to look up to. The stories I had heard about Lonzo before being lucky enough to move into his homo mansion were quite sad. I mean, not sad enough to give him any redeeming qualities, but sad nonetheless.

"If your fucking jaw gets to hurting and you feel like you can't suck another dick, just remember who the fuck your daddy is and get back to sucking." His eyebrow raised over a pair of fake diamond studded white sunglasses.

"You bitches better stretch those assholes wide, better not lock up that back door like you're some high and mighty ass bitch."

His two big henchmen tried fighting back laughter as they towered behind him.

"There's going to be a lot of fresh new tricks rolling into town looking for a salad bar. You best serve those out-of-town piggies what they paid for." Lonzo was referring to the new stadium opening up off of Zen mark circle. The city had been building it for the past three years, it was having it grand opening tonight with some hockey game taking place.

After Lonzo finished his inspiring pep-talk, he held out his long alien looking fingers for each of us to kiss the ring he got cheap at a pawn shop. When he made his way to me, I could feel his eyes burning through my very soul. He wanted me in a ditch somewhere far away, only he would not have it done himself,

"Maybe you'll get lucky tonight" he would say with a twisted smirk.

Nicholas started whispering to Jordan the second Lonzo and his henchmen shut the door behind them. Nicholas had Lonzo's dick down his throat so much he felt as if his mouth was reserved parking.

"There's just nothing out there that compares to Lonzo" he would say with a snobby grin. I looked over while sliding on my shoes to see Kenny standing in the corner eyeballing Nicholas. He looked like a lion hiding in the grass, ready to pounce on his unsuspecting prey.

"I'm taking Jericho Street tonight, bitches, So if any of you come sniffing around, I'm going straight to Lonzo" Nicholas proclaimed loudly. He looked over at me and smirked, he knew that was my corner.

"So, you're corner poaching now, Nic?" I asked getting to my feet. He looked up at me from the bed he sat cross legged on, his eyes like a retarded pug.

"I'm the top earner here, Gavin. I pick where I want to go. If there's a problem, I'm sure Lonzo would love to hear it." he stood up as if he was about to walk to the bedroom door. He was like a fucking child going to tattle because I said a bad word.

"Where the fuck do you think you're going, fatty?" Kenny stepped in Nicholas's way, his eyes burning with hatred.

"Get out of my way creep Kenny. Lonzo's going to hear about this as well" his voice so high pitched and whiney.

"You going to tell daddy Lonzo? How are you going to talk when your fucking jaw is wired shut fat boy?" Kenny growled like a hungry animal. Something about it turned me the fuck on.

"You fucking touch me and it will be the last thing you do!" Nicholas's voice hit an even higher pitch. He was moments from tears.

"Sit your fat ass back on the bed before I smear your face all over the fucking wall." Kenny took a step forward as he made his threat. Nicholas stumbled back, landing on the bed.

"You're in so much fucking trouble!" Nicholas cried out, tears now running down his fat little face.

"Jericho is yours" Kenny said giving me a wink.

"Thanks" was all I could muster. Something about Kenny punking out Nicholas, it was hot.

Walking down the street I thought about the ramifications of Kenny's actions. How would they play out when Nicholas ran and told Lonzo? I tried to push that in the back of my mind. The only thing I could really think about now was why was Creepy Kenny suddenly so fucking hot? I mean, he was always attractive, but holy shit. My dick got rock solid after that wink.

"You're not like the rest of these fucks, are you?" I remember Kenny asking me the day he came to the house. It was probably because I dressed like a man, or maybe more closely to a confused teenage lesbian. Regardless, I didn't share the same love for this profession that for some reason the others did.

"Got anything on you, guy?" a voice called out from the car riding slowly behind me. I turned slightly to see a white limo, the streetlights reflecting off its polished coat. A man... no maybe a teenager? I could not really tell, he seemed young, young enough that this could be his limo to prom or some shit.

"Sorry, the drugs come along with the other thing I'm selling. I promise you're not interested in that." I turned my head, laughing under my breath.

"How do you know that I don't want what else you're selling?" he called out again. Jesus, I was going to have to tell this kid to just fuck off.

"Go back home to mommy and daddy, little guy. I don't fuck anyone who can't even buy their own alcohol." the limo stopped, the back door opened and out stepped the kid.

"You assume I'm some kid?" I looked him up and down, he wore a white tuxedo with a pink flower attached on the upper left breast.

"It kind of looks like you're on your way to the middle school dance" I said full blown laughing at this point.

"Don't laugh at me, it's not polite to laugh at someone you just met." He crossed his arms as if I had offended him.

"Look kid, I'm sorry. I have a long night ahead of me. I promise wherever you're going is a lot more fun than where I'm heading." I was trying desperately to shake this poor kid. All I needed was for one of Lonzo's henchmen to pull up and see me not offering services and I would find myself picking up mine and this boy's teeth.

"Get in the limo, my driver and I will take you where you're going." The offer was appealing obviously but I just could not do it.

"Look kid, I appreciate it, but I can't be seen with someone who isn't a customer. Thank you for the offer, but I need to get on my way."

The kid stared at me for a moment, he looked frustrated like he was not accustomed to being told no. "Why do you people always put up a fight? Just once get in the fucking limo!"

His fists were clenched, his blond curls bounced off his brow as he shook his head in disappointment.

"You should go home and go to bed little fella" I said not feeling very threatened by his little tantrum. The wind blew and a very disgusting smell filled my nostrils, it smelled like death times ten.

"What in the hell is that?" I asked covering my nose with my shirt sleeve. A sharp pain went straight through my body like a bolt of lightning, I fell straight down on my face.

"Wake up, sleepy head. You're going to miss all the fun" I heard that kids voice in my head like he was taunting me. Everything was a blur at first, there were flashing lights, little girls in pretty dresses, that boy was dancing with them. "You're going to sleep the night away, why didn't you just get in the limo?"

Was he in front of me? What was going on? Was I moving?

"Where…What happened?" I asked with a dry mouth and a splitting headache.

"Yay you are finally awake! I thought I was going to have to poke you in the leg with a needle or something" That kids high pitched fucking voice cracked my skull like a winter log.

"Am I in your limo?" I asked rubbing my head, that damn smell was back.

"Yeah, you just fainted on the ground so I had my driver scoop you up like some strawberry ice cream and put you where the party is." Even half-conscious, I could tell this kid was a few cocks shy of an orgy.

Through my still cloudy vision, I could see other people sitting in the side row seats. They looked like they were dressed for prom as well. The strobe lights and the song 'Lick it up' was blaring almost too loud for me to even make out what the kid was saying.

"I want to introduce you to some of my close friends. We're on our way to the dance."

I did not have time for this bullshit, I had to get out of here.

"Cameron, I told you to slow down on the champagne, you know what that shit does to you." The boy laughed. Oddly, the boy and the music were the only ones making any noise. A limo full of kids should be an absolute noise nightmare. After a moment more my vison finally came into focus, what I saw made me wish it had not.

CHAPTER 5: PINK COTTON CANDY

"What in the fuck is going on, kid?" I asked with my eyes as wide as my gaping mouth. He looked at his friends and then back at me as if he were confused or did not know exactly how to answer my question.

"I told you that we're on the way to a dance. Do you not remember that?" He shook his head at me, smiling. Not counting myself and the psycho blond kid, the were five others sharing the back of this party limo, they were all dead.

"Your friends are rotting corpses, kid" I yelled over the music. He looked frustrated, "Henry can you please turn down the music?" he yelled up at the driver, to whom I had still yet to be introduced. The music faded slowly, to the point where you had to actually try to hear it. "Now what were you saying buddy?" the kid asked smiling at me, his smile was the most terrifying smile I had ever seen.

"You do realize that all of these kids are dead, right?" I asked looking around at the decomposed children.

"Well, you try getting through middle school and then trying to find the time for fun. You'd be dead on your feet as well." He smiled and raised the champagne glass in his hand like he was going to toast. The smell was building up to the point that it was making me sick.

How in the hell could this kid not smell that? Or he did smell it but did not care?

The bodies looked a week or so old. I was not an expert on the matter, but I had seen a movie once where it showed this autopsy scene of a dead prostitute.

She had been dead for a week and a half, her skin a mix of unpleasant colors. It was sad to see these kids cut down at such a young age, they had yet to experience this shit world and all it had to offer. I could not condemn them because I was handed a shitty deal. They could have grown up to fix the world, do something that mattered. The kid sat sown at the end, his arm around a girl that did not look like she had been dead as long as the others. She still had a shade of pink to her cheeks.

"This is my current girlfriend, Faith. I say current because who knows who I'll be interested in next week." He winked at me and laughed.

I could not tell if this kid was fucking with me or not. Like, he had to know this was bat shit insane. Riding around in a limo with the dead bodies of his friends… Where were the adults in this situation? Were there worried parents out there wondering where their missing kids are?

"So where is this dance you're going to?" I asked trying to amuse him. "Seems kind of late for a school dance if you ask me" I added. The kid looked at me and then out the tinted window, something was going on in his head, it was like watching a bi-polar person switch moods in an instant.

"The fucking dance is over, bro. This is the after party." He threw back his glass of champagne like it was a shot of tequila.

"I thought you said we were on the way to the dance?" I asked curiously.

"Well, what you think does not really fucking matter, does it?! This is my fucking party, and we will do what I want to do!" he screamed at me pointing his finger. I was taken back by his outburst, so taken back that I sat back further in my seat.

"You fucking people are always saying the same shit. How old are you? What is with the dead bodies? Where are we really going? You are all the same!" he screamed at the top of his lungs.

"Well, this has been a blast and I really appreciate it, but I think I'm ready to head home." I tried to sound like I was not scared out of my fucking mind.

"You want to know a secret?" he asked completely dismissing my plea.

"To be honest, kid, I just want the fuck out of this limo and away from you" I said defensively. Once again it seemed like he was ignoring anything I said.

"I'm a virgin" he said quietly like one of his dead friends were going to hear

46

him. "I know that must come as a complete shock to you considering how handsome and successful I am, but I guess I just haven't found the right one yet." I couldn't believe what this kid was saying, not the fact that he had never had underaged sex, that was his only redeeming quality in my book, it was the fact that he seemed so disconnected from reality.

"Um, well kid, I have to say I'm totally shocked that a looker like yourself hasn't went all the way with some lucky girl, but I'm sure your time will come when you're a little older."

He looked at me with ice cold eyes. I couldn't tell if he was about to lash out again, or cry. "Would you mind watching me on my first time? It would really mean a lot to me. No one has ever given me advice before." His question made me shift uncomfortably in me seat. What in the hell was I supposed to say to that?

"Kid I don't think you want anyone else there during that special time. It would probably ruin the magic if I'm being honest." My mouth was getting dryer and dryer every extra second I spent in this limo of death.

"If I fucking say be there, you'll fucking be there goddamn it!" he screamed at me as he tried to stand up. "Now who do you think would be a good first?" He looked at me and then at the row of dead girls.

"Um, you want one of these girls to be your first?" I asked understandably concerned.

"What is wrong with these girls? They're my age and are willing. I wouldn't be taking advantage of them if that's what you're thinking in that sick mind of yours, you pink haired freak!" He edged closer to me, his face twisted with anger.

I leaned back as far as the seat would allow me. "I didn't mean anything by it, kid. I just figured that you shouldn't settle for something so easy." I bit my lip before anything else came out. I had probably already offended him again.

"You know what? You are absolutely right. I should wait to dip my stick in a girl with a little more class." I felt slightly at ease, as at ease as one could possibly feel given the situation.

"Would you mind if I asked again where we are going? I mean, since the dance is not happening?" Why was I walking on eggshells with this little prick? I mean, yes, he was a psychopath, but he was still a little kid who did not look a day over thirteen.

"Henry likes to do laps around the block. We've passed the spot we picked you up three times now" he said holding his ribs with laughter.

I tried to peer through the window, the flashing strobe light made it impossible to see anything. While I was peering, I could have sworn the kid did something behind my back, his reflection in the window looked as if he were contorting his body like a possessed maniac. I turned around quickly but there he was just staring at one of the girls in a magenta-colored dress. Her hair looked like it may have been red at some point,. It was now matted down with clumps of dried mud and something sticky looking.

"Doesn't Samantha have the prettiest eyes you've ever seen on a girl?" he asked, touching her check with the back of his hand. I did not was not to look at the horror show in front of me, but I did notice that the poor girl only had one eye. It was a cloudy gray, hard to tell what color it had been before.

"Yep. Real pretty, kid" I felt like I was about to throw up, the smell got worse and worse the more the kid moved around the small space.

"Have you ever kissed a girl on her private parts?" the kid asked looking over at me.

"I can't say that I have" I said, closing my eyes. I rubbed my face again with my hands, I wanted to awake from this nightmare. Images of my face being held down into my mother's bare pussy flashed, my closed eyes would not protect me from that.

"Mommy likes to get drunk and pass out after I pump her full of my juice. Here, boy. Give it a taste." I could hear my fathers voice so clear I could have been on his lap. I opened my eyes to find no comfort. The kid was on his knees, his head under the dead girl's dress.

"What the fuck?!" I cried out in shock. It did not stop the kid from doing what he was doing.

"Her privates are so wet" the kid mumbled. I seized the opportunity to just get to my feet, shoving past him and out the back door. The car had been going a bit faster than I had anticipated. I hit the road face first, my body flipped twice before I came to a stop. The limo slammed on its breaks. The kid peeked his head out of the ajar back door, his mouth looked as if he had just eaten a melted dark chocolate candy bar.

"Fine, fuck you then." He slammed the door, and after a few seconds, the limo peeled off.

"What in the fuck!" I screamed as loud as I could. Where was I? Why couldn't I see out of my left eye? I softly wiped my face; my vison was a cloudy red. "Damn it" I mumbled. My face was caked in blood. The pat few weeks after the Spaniard incident had been normal for the most part, tonight was the end of that.

I pushed myself to my feet, my knuckles were peeled and bloody. "Where the fuck? what fucking street is this?" I called out. I took a harder hit to the head than I thought, this place was not familiar at all.

"Hello?" I called out to no answer, not even the sound of a stray cat on a trashcan. The street was dark and empty, the buildings around it were even darker. "Hello!?" I called out again, not even answered from an echo.

"You lost friend?" A voice behind me made me lunge forward in surprise. "Sorry to scare you, Gavin" an old man reached out his hand to pat me softly on the back.

"How do you know my name? Who are you?" I felt as If I had seen this old man somewhere before, I could not place his face.

"We've met before friend, outside the shelter a few weeks ago." I thought for a moment, I did not remember ever meeting this guy.

"I don't remember you. Sorry, but things have been kind of crazy lately."

He nodded his head like he understood. "Life can be like that sometimes. We just have to take it a day at a time." The old man's voice was oddly comforting.

"I really appreciate the advice sir, but do you have any clue where I am and how to get back to Jericho Street? I have had a night you would not believe." I felt bad just brushing the old man's advice off, but all I wanted was to get some where I recognized.

"Sorry, sometimes I ramble on and don't even realize it. I'll point you in the right direction." A wave of comfort swept over me, a feeling that I had never really felt in my life.

"Thank you so much!" I leaned forward and hugged this stranger. "Sorry about that, just excited is all." The old man just stared at me with a genuine smile, his eyes bluer than anything I had ever seen.

"It's okay, Gavin. You're just ready to get home, and I understand that. The name's Raguel." He extended his wrinkled hand.

"I'm Gavin White. It's good to meet you again, sir." I wish I could have remembered when I had met him before, with eyes like that how could I have forgotten this guy?

"Sir, you say we've met before, but honestly I just don't remember." I felt terrible that I could not remember him. He was being so kind and helpful, the least I could do was remember the one other time we had met.

"I promise it's no problem. You've had a lot on your plate, no time to be thinking about some strange old man you met once." He put his hand on my back and guided me down the street. "You don't want to be here anyway. This isn't a good place for someone like you to be in" the old man said shaking his head.

"What do you mean someone like me?" I asked defensively.

"I just mean that this area is for thieves and murderers, the ones that couldn't be saved" Once again, I felt bad. I had just jumped down this man's throat because I thought he was referring to my sexuality. There those blue eyes were again, it was like staring into the galaxy beyond the galaxy. They were ice blue diamonds sparkling through the darkness.

"If you don't mind me asking, sir. Are those contacts, or is that your actual eye color?" I asked stopping to stare into them once more.

He smiled a comforting smile "They are real, the only part of me that decided to not get old." He chuckled at his joke, it was hard not to do it back.

"Believe it or not, my actual hair color isn't pink" I joked with him back, we laughed together like old friends. It was strange that I found myself forgetting that I was in some strange part of town that I did not recognize. Raguel made every second in his presence feel like a safe place. My stomach growled like an angry lion, even Lonzo's beef stew sounded appealing at this point.

"Where did you need to be tonight, Gavin?" he asked as we began walking once more.

"I need to get to Jericho Street, if possible. I don't know how far we are from it, to be honest. I've never actually seen this part of town. Can I bum a ride from you?" I asked feeling hopeful.

"I don't have a car, nor a license. Never have in this life" I looked over at him in surprise. I mean, there were a lot of people in the city that didn't own a car due to the inconvenience of parking, but this guy had to be in his eighties. How had he made it without at least a license?

"Well, do you live around here?" I wanted to know more about Raguel and his life. I found him to be the most interesting person I had ever met.

"I've spent most of my life on the move, it's difficult for me to remain in one place for long." His response only made me more curious.

"Are you a drifter? Did you ride in on a train or something?" Before he could answer, I looked up at a street sign, it was Jericho Street.

"How?" I asked looking around. How in the hell did we end up back here so quick? Had we walked that far? This made no sense.

"Time sure does fly when you're having fun, doesn't it?" the old man asked, resting his hand on my shoulder.

Normally I was not the type who was very fond of unnecessary touching, not unless I was getting paid for it. There was just something about Raguel that made it no big deal. I looked back in the direction we came, the road all looked familiar, the same road I had seen on countless nights of standing here waiting on the next slow-moving car to pull up.

"I have a million questions" I blurted out suddenly like he was just going to vanish into thin air. Raguel smiled at me; those blue eyes were enough to put you into a mindless trance for hours.

"I will see you again, Gavin. I'm sure of it." He patted my arm, gave me a kind wink, then walked away back to where we had just come from. I wanted to shout out for him to come back. I wanted to know more about this stranger. I just stood there silently.

"You sell ass or what?" a voice yelled out from a parked car behind me. I turned to see a beat-up blue Toyota parked on the side of the street directly under the lamp.

"You have to by one to get the other, sweetie" I answered, trying to put my game face back on. I hated calling these slime balls sweetie, honey, and all that other shit.

"Well, if you got some x on you, I'll pop it in my mouth while my dick's in yours." I felt around my pocket for a moment. Lonzo always had us carry a bit of Ecstasy, coke, and a small variety of different pain pills. To me it seemed like a good way to get us robbed or killed. Most pimps had their thugs keep an eye on the workers. Lonzo always said "You think I'm going to pay mother fuckers to babysit? You lose any of my shit or cost me money, I will stitch up your mouth and ass hole, so you never make money again." I rolled my eye's hearing his voice in my head.

I heard another car turning the street corner. My gut tightened, thinking it was going to be that long white limo again. "You coming or not? You are not the only mouth on these streets, Pinky." I turned back to the man in the Toyota he was not bad looking, a blonde with a scruffy beard and a half-burnt cigarette hanging from his lips.

An hour later I was still rinsing my mouth out. That guy had not showered in what smelled like a few days. You just have to smile and play like the are the most handsome thing you had ever sucked off. The back of my neck was sore from his constant pushing. I tossed the empty water bottle into the open dumpster next to the alley, a stray cat scared the shit out of me when it jumped out. A small crowd of people walked past me dressed like they were on the way to a nightclub, they were loud and obnoxious. The typical sewer rats that polluted this city.

"Have you been there before?" A man in a leather jacket asked a short petite woman walking next to him.

"No this is my first time. I've heard it gets pretty wild" she responded. It was not hard to guess that they were talking about club Dumitru's around the block. It was a goth themed nightclub where all the wannabe vampires and wrist-slitters went to drink red wine and pretend it was blood.

"I heard that they serve you pigs blood mixed in a daiquiri" the small girl said giggling. I shook my head while rolling my eyes. People could be so fucking stupid.

Lonzo made Nicholas work the outside of club Dumitru's once. He only lasted a few hours before the bouncers beat the piss out of him, taking his drugs and money for their trouble.

"You on your way to the club as well?" a voice asked from the street. I looked over to see a tall slender man wearing a long black trench coat, his black hair slicked to the side, his skin ghostly white.

"No, that's not really my scene" I answered, looking around for the group of friends for whom he was probably waiting.

"Not your scene huh?" he asked smiling. His teeth like expensive pearls in the jewelry store window.

"Yeah, I'm not really into the goth scene. I mean, I'm gay and all but even that shit is too gay for me." I laughed awkwardly like the man was going to be offended.

"To each his own, I guess" he said quietly after a few moments. His eyes like bottomless pits.

"I see you're dressed for the part though. You have this count Dracula thing going on." I walked a little closer to him, he was even taller than he looked from afar.

"Dracula thing?" he asked raising one of his dark pointed eyebrows.Did this guy not intentionally dress like a fucking vampire? Was he going to start laughing anytime soon?

"I mean no offense, but you look like a vampire. You are pale as shit, your fingernails are long, the black coat. Was that not what you were going for?" I asked curiously.

He rested both hands in front of himself, his long fingers intertwining like sleeping snakes. He stared at me for what seemed like forever. Either he was bad with comebacks, or he was trying to figure out which part of me to suck on first.

"Why not accompany me to the night club? We can discus Vampires and the boogeyman on the way" he asked pointing his hand in the direction of Dumitru's.

"Sorry, I have work to do. Maybe catch me some other time." His eyes lit up and a sharp smile slid across his face like a vicious centipede.

"Catch you some other time" he repeated. His eyes like a cat in the dark. Suddenly another obnoxious crowd of people passed in front of the tall man.

He seemed to disappear into the chaos.

"What in the fuck was up with that dude?" I asked myself. Sadly, that was not the weirdest thing to happen tonight. After a few more hours of jaw tiring blowjobs, I started back for the house. I would have sucked a hundred dicks over going back to that bucket of piss called home. I know that any normal person would be freaked the fuck out by all the weird shit that had been happening lately. The Spaniard, the boy in the limo, the creepy vampire nutjob, but after a lifetime of misery and shit, everything, including the strange, became that much more normal. Laying on the floor that night I tried once more to black out the pictures of the past. Only they were not pictures, they were full length VHS tapes that could not be fast forwarded.

* * *

"Where are we going to go, Gavin?" My little brother whispered as he shoved his little face into my stomach. He hugged me so tightly that it would have taken two grown men to pull him away.

"I don't know, bud. We'll find out soon. I won't let them split us up."

Him hearing the words ;split up' made him squeeze even tighter.

"I don't want them to take you away from me, Gavin. Please don't let them."

My eyes filled with tears, they were like acid burring my cheeks.

"I'm not going anywhere that you're not going as well" I said, patting him on the head. His grip loosened up a bit. "Come on, Keith. We need to start packing" I said guiding him to his bedroom down the hall. As we walked past my parents' bedroom, I shielded Keith's eyes, he did not need to see the horror behind the caution tape.

"Just keep looking ahead, buddy. Don't worry about anything else."

He held my sweaty hand as we both marched forward. "What happened to mommy?" he asked sitting on his bed while I packed the clothes from his top drawer into a small suitcase.

"Mommy was sick, buddy. She was so sick that fell asleep and didn't wake up."

I did not know how to explain what happened. The woman in the navy-blue sports coat didn't seem to care enough to explain the situation in a way Keith would understand.

"Will she never wake up?" Keith asked holding onto a small horse I had carved for him in Mr. Heads shop class.

"No bud, she's not going to wake up" I fought with myself not to cry, I did not want to do that in front of Keith. I needed to be strong for him. "Is there anything else you want to bring, little dude?" I asked smiling up at him from the floor.

He looked around for a moment, then handed me the wooden horse. "Obviously, we can't forget sir gallops" I said, taking the horse with a smile. "It's all going to get better Keith, I promise" I said, doing my best imitation of a horse voice. Keith laughed hysterically; I smiled the most genuine smile.

"It's time to go, boys" the social worker shouted down the hall.

"I don't like that lady very much" Keith whispered in my ear. I patted him on the back

"Let's just make nice and put up with her for now buddy. She isn't any worse than we're used to." Keith nodded his head as we walked back down the hall.

* * *

I jumped up when something rubbed against my foot. Normally, I wouldn't pay it any mind. Probably as rat or something... This was no rat.

"What the fuck are you doing, Jordan?" I asked squinting in the dark room. Jordan was crouched down by my feet digging through a black trash bag, my black trash bag.

"Sorry, Gavin. I thought I dropped something" he stammered, obviously lying.

"How the fuck do you drop something into a trash bag full of clothes that was high up in the closet? Answer me that, you fucking thief!"

I lunged forward before he could come up with another lie. "What were you trying to take, goddamnit?" I screamed as I wrapped my hands around his scrawny neck. By this time, the rest of the room was awake and watching the excitement.

"Looks like Jordan got caught again" called out Nicholas from his bed.

"I didn't take anything yet, Gavin. I swear." He gagged and coughed after I let go.

"Did you not make enough money tonight, so you try to steal mine?" I asked kicking him as I got to my feet.

"It's not like that, Gavin. I swear it" he begged putting his hands up to block his before and after meth poster face.

"Touch my shit again bitch, and I'll slit your fucking throat" I yelled, kicking him one more time.

"Should I just go ahead and do that for you?" Kenny asked with a smile.

There goes Kenny again with this looking hot bullshit, even out of a dead sleep he looked like a Greek statue.

"No, it's all good. Maybe next time" I said, smiling back.

"Gaaaaay" Nicholas called out. The others started laughing like a wild pack of gay hyenas.

"Shut the fuck up!" Kenny demanded; the laughing stopped as quick as it started. I looked though my bag to make sure nothing was missing, all my worthless shit was still there. I thought back on the dream I was having before the Jordan incident. I thought about Keith. "Don't let them split us up, Gavin." I heard his voice call out like he was lying right next to me.

"I'm sorry buddy" I whispered to myself as one tear rolled down my face, dripping on the floor.

CHAPTER 6: SUGAR SWEET SLIT

"Holy fucking shit! Did you bitches hear what happened late last night at that stupid fucking goth club over off of Jericho?"

That was the first thing I heard as I sat up off the floor, the sound of a bunch of gays gossiping like school girls. Nicholas took another big meaty bite of Lonzo's famous beef stew.

"Apparently the place got shot up, like fucking shot to shit." For the first time ever, I was interested in hearing the gossip, especially since it was about the club that I was invited to by some weird freak in a trench coat.

"The news said that late in the night some psycho bolted all the doors shut from the inside and then went on a shooting spree. He killed like thirty people or some shit."

I walked out into the hall where the conversation was taking place, only to get met with about three judgmental bitch stares.

"We're just talking, Gavin. Scurry along, we know its not your thing" Nicholas teased, laughing with Jordan and Gilly.

"Are you talking about Dumitru's club?" I asked leaning against the door frame. They all looked at each other and then back at me.

"What about it, cotton candy gay?" Nicholas joked, trying to keep a straight face. I shook my head in frustration. I was a bit stuck up, maybe I should laugh a little more.

"Was the fucking news talking about Dumitru's club or not, goddamnit!?" I shouted, grabbing Nicholas by the collar of his baby-blue polo.

"Jesus, calm down she hulk. I was only joking" Nicholas pushed me off then patted down his now wrinkled polo. "Yeah, they were fucking talking about that freak show club. Someone shot the place up, big whoop" Nicholas said, rolling his eye's and turning to walk off down the hall. I stood there for a moment trying to process the information.

Holy fuck! What if I had gone with that man? Did he get shot? Did he do the shooting? I had so many questions.

"Hey... um, Gavin. Look man, I'm sorry about last night." I looked over at a puppy eyed Jordan. He looked sorry, but the truth was he was just sorry I had caught his druggy ass.

"Get the fuck away from me Jordan" I demanded, not even looking at him in the eye anymore.

"Little pink gay" a voice belonging to one of Lonzo's henchmen called out as he walked down the hall towards the room. Of course he did not know mine or any other name in this house.

"I wonder if it's about last night" said Kenny as he slid on his black tank top "I got your back if it is" he said standing next me.

"Little pink gay boy, you have mail." The big moron stuck out his gigantic hand, in it was a white envelope. I looked up at the henchmen, it was strange seeing him without his twin.

"I've never gotten mail here before. How would anyone know where to send me a letter?" I asked the brooding henchman.

"Not my concern, Lonzo says don't let it happen again or I am to break your jaw."

I nodded my head to let him know I understood.

"Who the hell could it be from?" Kenny asked looking down at the words 'Gavin White' written in pink crayon.

"Looks like a second grader wants to be your pen-pal" Kenny laughed, slapping me on the ass.

"What the hell was that for?" I asked looking at him as he walked out of the room behind the henchman.

"Just felt like doing it" he winked with a smile. As excited as I was about that little ass slap, I was more focused on the unopened envelope still in my hand. I sat down on the edge of Gilly's bed. I slowly tore the flap open, inside was to no surprise, a letter...

* * *

Dear Gavin,

I hope you are well my friend; I hope that you are in good health and that you are living the life you much deserve. I have not been in the best of health. I am missing a chunk from the side of my face due to an unfortunate incident involving a drill.

That line made me almost slide off the bed and onto my skinny ass, how in the hell did he find me? Why was he writing me a fucking letter and not just coming to murder me in my sleep? I should take this letter to the police. They're looking for the Spaniard now. After that night in the motel, I had not heard anything about anyone involved, maybe the police were having trouble locating me to give me any news. I looked back down at the poorly written crayon written letter.

I am sure you know about the one in reference... I am writing you to let you know that I feel terrible about what I had planned to do to you. It was wrong of me to not just kill you quickly. I shouldn't have tried to torture you for the crimes of another, you stayed strong and fought back which I understand completely. But in doing so, you have disfigured me so badly that no man women or child will ever fuck me again. You have ruined my life, Gavin. My mother always said I had a very handsome face... now that has been taken from me. If you had just died that night, I wouldn't look like this. I wouldn't be this deformed freak. I have taken up residency close by the whore house where you sit and read this letter. I want my pound of flesh, Gavin; it is only fair that you give it to me. If you take this letter to the police, they will just try to lock me away again. They were not incredibly pleased with me after I raped and beat that prison guard to death. I suppose they want me even more so now. Gavin, if you find me and let me take from you what you have taken from me, I promise that I will leave your brother Keith and his family alone. I will NOT go to their big beautiful house on the far outskirts of Moon city and rape your two young nieces in front of each other. I will NOT bash your sister-in-law's head in with the hammer in my tool box. And lastly, I will NOT cut your brothers head off and feed his wind pipe to that little white dog they have out back. None of this will happen if you can find me within two days of that big ogre handing you this letter and offer me what you have stolen. I know it would be so much easier for me to walk down the street, climb up to your bedroom window and get you myself, but where is the fun in that? Come find me, my dead friend. I hope you are at peace in life. See you soon.

Signed... what was it you called me to the police? Some raciest unfriendly name, oh yes...

, The Spaniard

* * *

The room around me spun like I had just taken a shot of heroin straight to the brain. How in the hell did he know about my brother and his family? My little brother that got out of Moon City and made something out of nothing. My flesh and blood.

I tried to stand up but could not, my legs wobbled, the room was still doing cartwheels, my hands were too sweaty to grab the beds headboard and pull myself up.

"Gavin? Are you feeling, ok?" Kenny asked sitting down next to me on the bed. I could not get the words out. I stammered and stuttered like I had been dropped on my head as a kid.

"He knows. He knows where" was all I could get out before vomiting all over the bedroom floor.

"Shit, Gavin. You need some help." Kenny sounded concerned as he rubbed my back. "Now tell me what's going on. Maybe I can help."

I shoved him with my free hand "Don't" was all I could say with my mouth, my eyes on the other hand told him a horrific tale of fear and loss.

"Calm down and breathe. Tell me what I can do, and I'll do it." He returned, rubbing my back, even though I had pushed him away already.

"I have to find the man who sent this letter. I have to find him in two days or he's going to kill my brother" I spat it out like I did the vomit a few seconds ago.

Kenny grabbed the letter from my hand, ripping the bottom corner off due to the karate tight grip I had on it. I watched his eyes skim every line, every demand, every promise.

"I know in our line of work going to the police is about as pointless as cocks on a turtle shell, but we have to show them this, now." He went to stand up, but I grabbed tightly to his forearm.

"No! You don't know what this guy is capable of. This mother fucker knows every move I make, every person I come in contact with. He knows things that I've never said to anyone."

The thought of Keith and his family sitting down for dinner, his wife Janet smiling at him from across the table as she scoops macaroni and cheese from a bowl onto the plates in front of Kimmy and Gale. I had never seen this before, but I knew that was the life that my brother was now living. I pictured him everyday sitting in that big office making phone calls, being an important person to everyone around him.

"I need to know where Lonzo's henchman got this letter" I said to Kenny with my eyes burning red with pure fury.

"I don't think Lonzo, or his men are going to talk to you, man. They have Nicholas and Gilly upstairs doing who knows what fucked up shit."

My fists clenched so tight that my knuckles popped. I could taste the blood in my mouth from squeezing my fucking teeth together.

"Those mother fuckers will talk, one way or another" I said finally getting to my feet. My sleeveless 'Legalize eating ass' t-shirt had spots of my vomit soaking into it. I had no fucking time to care, this shit was going to end.

"Do you have a gun, Kenny?" I asked grabbing him by the arm. For a few seconds, we stood there staring at each other without blinking an eye. It felt like we were reading each other's pain in that very moment.

"I have a straight razor I keep in my boot, but you need to think this through, Gavin. Don't make some crazy decision based on how you feel right now." He put both of his hands on my shoulders. "Let me help you think this through." He now had his warm hand rested on the side of my face. "Your shirt is hilarious by the way" he said with a smile, I could not help but smile back.

"Now, let's go up and talk to Lonzo together. Who knows, he might actually be able to help us." The idea sounded so damn good when Kenny was talking. I wish I hadn't just thrown up because- there it was, both hands on my face and a mouth full of tongue.

I grabbed a handful of that military cut hair as we slammed each other against the closet door. I could feel his cock getting hard under those tight jeans. He stuck his hand straight down my pants before I could do it first. Weirdly enough, in this extremely erotic moment, all I could think about was the fact that I had just thrown up, and now I had someone else's tongue down my throat.

Kenny did not seem to mind; he was way to busy pulling my cock from my pants. My heart raced, the blood pumped through my body like lava.

"Wow, what do we have here?" a voice only belonging to the most annoying shit stain fuck boy in this house asked as he pointed and laughed.

"Get fucking lost Nicholas!" Kenny shouted, still holding my hard dick firmly in his grasp.

"Or what, creepy Kenny? Are you going to bash my pussy in with a sledgehammer too?" Nicholas laughed harder and harder, soon everyone else started piling up behind him to do the same thing.

Kenny's grip on my cock grew increasingly painful. "Kenny you're going to have to loosen up or think about letting go" I said jokingly as I ignored the laughter. Kenny did not seem to be in a joking mood anymore, his face went from blood red to beat purple in a matter of seconds.

"Ignore these fucking idiots Kenny" I said, grabbing his face. His eyes were so blood shot that it looked like his head was about to explode. "Let's get the fuck out of here and never come back. We don't need Lonzo, and we certainly don't need this group of soft fucks."

He turned to look at the now smirking crowd of onlookers. "You mother fuckers are lucky I didn't slit your throats in your sleep."

Nicholas and Gilly looked at each other and then behind them at Jordan. It was like they were waiting on who was going to be the tough guy to defend them.

"You think you can just talk and act the way you want, creepy Kenny?"

Nicholas said puffing out his chest, his chest may have been full of balmy air, but his eyes were overflown with doubt.

"I should march my cute ass right up those steps and tell Lonzo all about your threats, and maybe even tell him about the free fucking going on between you two losers." Nicholas looked behind himself at Jordan and Gilly. They patted his shoulder in support.

Before I could blink Kenny flew across the room, a loud cracking sound sent a handful of teeth and blood flying into the wall. Jordan Stepped forward but a hard kick to his gut sent him flailing backwards into the hallway.

"Come here fucker" Kenny growled as he grabbed Jordan by his throat.

"Please don't, I'm sorry" Jordan begged, tears and snot ran down his face.

Before he could muster another plea for his life, Kenny hit him across the head with a mean right hook. The hit was so violent that Jordan's body folded sideways in mid-air before crumbling to the floor.

I tried to react, but it was all happening so fast, I knew I should say something, what if he killed one of them? "Kenny!" I shouted over the crying and sobbing of the beaten and battered whores.

Kenny was in the zone; he paid no mind to my pleas either. "Look at me you fat cock sucker!" He reached down, grabbing Nicholas by his shirt. He dragged his fat body with ease across the bedroom, the veins in his arms were as big as angry king cobras.

"Put your head right here, tubby." Kenny placed Nicholas's bloody face on the opened door frame. He lay there crying like a fat hungry baby.

"You hungry fat boy?!" Kenny screamed as he grabbed a hold of the thick wooden door.

"Kenny Don't!" I screamed in horror.

It was too late. Kenny slammed the door with so much force that it shook the walls of the bedroom, an old picture frame fell from the wall. The room was silent for a second, all I could hear was a faint ringing. I could see Jordan screaming as he crawled over to an unrecognizable Nicholas. I looked up at Kenny, his fist clenched, his chest going filling up then releasing the fire that had been burning him from the inside.

"Kenny, what in the hell did you just do?" I asked falling to my knees.

There was obviously no love lost on Nicholas's behalf, but this created another major problem in my life that needed as much as a hot woman with a wet pussy. I guess the stories about Kenny were true. I could see now that he was the type of person to get angry enough to beat his wife to death with a sledgehammer. A man who could brutalize someone like that with his bare hands, was surly capable of much worse.

"Shut that fucking crying up, Jordan. Gilly, get your fucking ass back in here!" Kenny pulled open the door, pulling a sickly faced Gilly over Nicholas's lifeless body. "Shut the fucking crying up you little bitches!" Kenny roared so loudly that a chill went down my spine. "This is what's going to happen, you little fags are going to get in the closet and keep your fucking mouths shut until Gavin and I are gone"

I looked over at him confused. Did he think I was about to run away with him? Pack our bags and catch the train? This man was fucking insane.

"I need to find the Spaniard. I can't run away with you, Kenny." Kenny turned only his head, his eyes still bloodshot and rabid.

"I did this for you, Gavin. Don't you see that? I cannot turn back from this! I thought we had something real."

Spit flew from his mouth like a pit-bull with rabies. I slowly put my hands up in defense, it was like having a hundred laser sights pointed at my chest.

"I didn't want this, Kenny. I just wanted to go and help my brother. None of this had to happen if you had just walked away."

His eyes went almost black, beads of sweat dripped from his head. "Do you have any idea how ungrateful you sound right now? I came to this shit hole house because I had nowhere else to go. The fucking police have been looking for me longer than I can even remember. You want me to be your hero, Gavin?" he had turned his full body towards me at this point, his dark gray shirt now drenched in blood and sweat.

"We have spoken to each other maybe one other time before today, Kenny. You don't know me and I don't know you. We had a hot moment, but it didn't mean what you thought it meant." I knew I was digging a deeper hole. I only hoped that if I stalled long enough, help would come barging through the door.

"So, you're saying that I mean nothing to you? You're too good for me? Is that it, Gavin?" Kenny started to move closer, the wall behind me left nowhere to run. "People like you are all the same. You come into my life, you pull my heart strings just enough to make me fall in love with you, then you stab me in the back." By this time, Kenny was just inches from my face.

"You're just another whore." A hard smack across my face brought the ringing sound back to full volume, I fell back against the wall with a thud.

"I did not want to do that, Gavin! Why did you make me to that to you!?" Kenny was leaning down screaming, strings of warm spit sprinkling on my forehead. I looked up for just a moment to see the bottom of Kenny's boot connect with my mouth and nose, the sound of broken teeth and cartilage played a sleep-inducing melody.

* * *

I awoke from another beating. I lay there on the living room floor, my dads work boots seemed to catch my face from smacking the floor.

"We need to throw both of these little fuckers out on the streets, that'll teach them to man up and stop being a couple of sissy ass queers."

My fathers voice was the loudest thing these walls had heard, even they covered their ears to shut out the only constant.

"Did you have to smack him that hard? He asked to stay at a friend's house. I thought him being gone was what you wanted."

There was silence, I knew the look he was giving her as he stood there in the kitchen clenching tightly to a deep brown beer bottle.

"Bitch, don't you know he is just going to go over and have faggot sex with that boy? I don't need the boys laughing at me because my son decided he was going to be a fucking homo!" The sound of the bottle breaking on the floor meant that now my father had a free hand to do with what he pleased. My mother would say sorry and try to calm him down, or she would take the route of continuing to question his decision. Either way never seemed to work in her favor.

"Well, what do your friends think about all the sick things you do to your son? Do they know their favorite drinking friend is a perverted pedo-"

Before she could finish, there was the familiar pop that could only mean that his slap made contact.

"What the fuck did you say, bitch? Do you think you're some kind of big pussy badass now? This is my fucking house, and you will show me the fucking respect I deserve!"

I could hear her dazed body being dragged across the kitchen floor. The cigarette butt covered coffee table helped me get to me feet. I would be eighteen by tomorrow, I could legally walk the fuck out of this nightmare.

"Mommy?" I heard as I looked down the hall from the living room.

"Keith!" I called out.

"Mommy wasn't listening to daddy, Keith. She's going to make us dinner like the good wife and mother she is, isn't that right baby?" Keith nodded sadly at my father's words. There was a clicking sound, the sound I would soon find out was my father turning the front burner of the stove on.

"Let's wake mommy up so she knows we're hungry."

I could see Keith's eyes grow from dimes to half-dollars. The muffled scream of my mother as her face was pressed against the burner would haunt my dreams for the rest of my life.

"No daddy!" Keith cried out. I ran to him as fast as I could, snatching him up and running to the bedroom without looking back.

"It's okay buddy. I'm getting us out of here." I ran over to the bedroom window, a loud pounding on the bedroom door made Keith cry even harder.

"Open the fucking door, Gavin. No little faggot is going to be locking doors in my house, especially in my goddamn bedroom!" The pounding grew louder and louder.

"I'm going to count to fucking three and this bedroom door better open, or I'm going to kick it down and rip off your fucking head!"

I popped the two latches at the top of the window. I pulled with all my strength, it was painted fucking shut, how did I not remember that? The door cracked down the center, splinters of wood covered the carpet.

"Look at my fucking door you little fuck! Look what you made me do to my fucking door!" My father ran his shoulder into it once more before it completely came apart.

Not taking my eyes off him, I grabbed a large pair of scissors from my mother's vanity. Keith ran to my side, hugging tightly around my waist.

"Stay the fuck away from us you drunk pervert piece of white trash!" I screamed raising the scissors high in the air. My father stood there breathing heavy, his bright blue eyes piercing through me, his fat gut hanging out from his filthy, once white wife beater. The hair on his arms and shoulders covered in flakes of white paint and wood.

"What did you say, faggot?" he asked in a deep angry growl. I kept the big silver pair of scissors raised high. Part of me wanted so badly for him to fall over dead of a heart attack right then and there, but that was something I prayed for every night of my life.

"You heard me, mother fucker!" I screamed even louder than before.

"Please stop" my mother begged as she felt her way down the hallway. When she entered the room, the shear sight of her made Keith bury his face deeper into my hip.

"Leave my Keith out of it, please don't hurt him" my mother begged softly, the right side of her face looked like something from a horror movie I had seen at my friend Dillion's house a few years back.

"You called me a mother fucker, right?" my father asked taking a step back, the twisted smile he gave me was the only smile I had ever seen him make.

"You want to see how much of a mother fucker I am boy? Want me to show you how to fuck a pussy? This will straighten you up a bit."

My mother was pushed down on the bed. She looked up at me without ever breaking eye contact. "This is how you fuck pussy, fag boy."

My mother's blue jeans were ripped down violently to her ankles, her white underwear ripped off in a single yank.

"Don't get hard looking at my dick now, boy." My father laughed as he rammed himself inside her. He thrusted harder and harder, my mother and I never looked away from each other.

"Keep your face hidden buddy" I said, trying to hold one hand over Keith's exposed ear. My father grunted loudly as his pulled his dick out, cumming on my mother's bare ass. "See how I pulled out, boy? That shit prevents little bastards like you from happening. Best remember that."

My mother closed the one eye that she could, breaking the eye contact that saved me from having to fully watch what my father was doing, the nicest thing she had ever done for me.

"You want to watch me do the same thing to the brat, boy? You can keep eye contact with him to if it helps." My father's sick and twisted laugh echoed not only through this broken home but through what was left of my innocence.

"Come near him and I will fucking kill you, do you hear me? I will fucking kill you." The voice that my father heard wasn't the voice of a scared eighteen-year-old that was fighting to save his brother, but the voice of the monster that he created with his bare-hands.

"You- you better" he pointed his finger trying to say something. I could see his disgusting back hair prickle up like a ghost had just brushed past.

"I swear to god I will fucking kill you, dad. I will fucking kill you if you touch my brother." My voice was cold and dead, a voice belonging to the man I needed to become in this very instant. I pictured the large pair of scissors stabbing though his belly fat, I could hear his pathetic screams. My mother got to her feet, she stumbled out of the bedroom, cum running down her ass cheek.

"You get your shit and get the fuck out of my house" my father said, pointing at me once more. "You take him, and I'll call the police and tell them you kidnapped my son."

I felt Keith hug tighter and tighter hearing my father's threats. He turned and walked through the shattered door, pushing my mother over as he passed her in the hallway.

"Don't leave me, Gavin. Please, I'll do anything to just go with you."

I got down to one knee and wrapped my arms around the one good thing in this world. "After tonight, we won't have to live like this anymore, I promise"

* * *

A dimly lit light was far away in the darkness. It was the light of a happy place, a place where the Spaniard was dead, my brother was safe, and I stayed out in his big guest house temporarily while I worked on finishing college courses. The light started moving closer and closer. It knew how much I wanted it, so it decided to come to me instead. As the light drew closer and closer, I realized that it looked oddly familiar. I had spent countless hours staring up at this light, the remembered falling to the floor and seeing it before I went unconscious.

"Fuck." I sat up rubbing my head, it felt as if I had just had my ass beat.

"Watch Jordan. Watch you dirty fuck" I heard Kenny's voice. He was panting and out of breath. "Don't turn your head!" Kenny's voice grew louder and angrier.

"Please, I don't want to, Kenny" Jordan cried. Like an a slightly adjusted pair of binoculars, the room came into clear focus.

"What the Fuck are you doing, Kenny?" I asked shocked. He looked over at me, his eyes starting to roll back into his head, he was about to cum.

"Please make him stop, Gavin. Please make him stop" Jordan begged by my side, his face was beaten and swollen so badly that I could only tell it was him buy the disgusting meth sores. I looked back over at Kenny. He sat on the edge of Jordans bed, completely naked, covered in blood.

"Do you think it will come out of his throat, Gavin?" Kenny asked as he thrusted his bloody cock in and out of the gaping mouth hole on Gilly's decapitated head. "Fuck I'm about to cum." His body tensed up. He leaned his head backwards as the veins in his neck bulged.

"Oh, fuck baby" he leaned back on the bed exhausted. The decapitated head bounced on the floor, slightly rolling under the bed. "I made my ex-wife do something similar after I smashed her pussy with that hammer. I cut her in half with a handsaw, then fucked her bottom half as I carried it around the house with me." Kenny leaned forward, taking Jordan's pillow and wiping the blood from his limp cock on it.

"After I used her torso as a fuck doll for a few days, I tossed it over the fence to the neighbor's dog. He ate most of it before my neighbor ended up finding Sammy with a mouth full of cum crusted asshole." Knowing that

Kenny was telling the truth about what he had done to his wife made my stomach wrench.

Next to me J,ordan cried harder and harder. For once, I felt sorry for him.

"Shut your cum hole Jordan, before my dick finds it's way in there" Kenny said laughing. "You know it's kind of crazy to think we've had all this fun down here and it's about that time where Lonzo comes down to give us his little pep talk on how to slang dick" Kenny looked over at the half-opened door with an excited smile.

"You know, when Lonzo see's what you've done, he's going to have his men kill you" I said, still rubbing the gash on my swollen lip. Kenny looked down at me, that excited smile still on his face, he was like a kid on Christmas.

"Are you going to kill three people, armed with guns, with the fucking straight razor you used to cut Gilly's head off?"

His smile faded just a bit after my thought-provoking question. "You know, Gavin. It's a shame that you'll never get to save that little brother of yours. I would love to watch that Spaniard guy do his work on that cute little family."

I felt that rage start to build back in my gut, that rage that I needed to dig up to protect Keith at all costs.

"These hoe's best be ready, because we need that cash flow about now." I heard Lonzo talking to his henchmen as the three of them walked down the stairs from his luxury penthouse.

"Looks like its about that time, lover" Kenny said getting to his feet, still naked. He picked the bloody straight razor up from the floor. "Quickly, Gavin. Who do you think will get the killing shot? I bet it will be Lonzo since he likes being front and center" he laughed as he did a little dance around Gilly's severed head.

"What in the fuck happened?" I heard Lonzo ask his men in the hallway. Lonzo must have gotten close enough to see Nicholas's smashed in head peaking out from the door.

"It looks like Jordan sir" one of the twins replied in amazement, or shock. It was hard to tell.

"No shit, its Nicholas, dumb fuck."

The door was quickly kicked the rest of the way open, Lonzo and his two henchmen stood there taking in all the horror's that this room now had to offer.

"Time for our pep talk?" asked Kenny, still dancing around the severed head.

"Lonzo, please help me!" Jordan cried out as he scrambled to his feet. Before he took the first step in Lonzo's direction, Kenny swiped hard and fast. The blade of the straight razor like a flash of silver colored light. For a moment, I thought that Kenny had only swung the razor to deter Jordan from taking another step, only I was wrong.

"What the fuck!?" shouted Lonzo as Jordan dropped to his knees, grasping at the giant gash in his throat. Before I could turn to look back at Lonzo's reaction there was an explosion of gun fire coming from three aimed pistols. Blood spattered all over me like an exploding water balloon, both of my ears ringing once again.

Kenny dropped down on the floor in front of me, his body folded like a broken accordion.

"Which one do you think got me, Gavin?" he asked as a pool of blood seeped from his mouth; his eye's rolled back into his head.

"What in the fuck went on in here Pinky?!" Lonzo asked, throwing his pistol down on the bed.

"Kenny, he freaked the fuck out and started attacking all of us. I don't know why."

In retrospect, I wasn't lying.

"This shit needs to be cleaned up before the day shift bitches get home to see it."

Lonzo snapped his fingers, the twins got to work like they had done this a hundred times.

"Lonzo, I need to talk to you" I said getting to my feet. Lonzo looked over at me with a mix of emotions. He nodded his head, directing me upstairs. When he turned, I quickly slid the straight razor into my sock, hopefully I would not need it.

CHAPTER 7: MOON CITY

I would not say that I was necessarily shocked by the fact that Lonzo's penthouse was way over hyped, but it was surprising. My eye's darted left to right, up and down. I mean it was a lot nicer than any other room in this shit hole, that I was certain of. The king-sized bed was draped in purple silk sheets, the walls were plastered in this gaudy gold wallpaper, a glowing pink light from a lava lamp in the far corner. I looked down at my feet, the carpet was a thick purple rug that looked like someone had shot and skinned barney the dinosaur. This room was a painful reminder of a time twenty years past.

"Is it everything you dreamed of pinky?" Lonzo asked, pouring a glass of what I could only assume was scotch. I mean, as high class as he pretended to be.

"You need this more than I do right now." He handed me to glass, the light brown liquid burned my nostrils. I was not a drinker; I just never had a taste for alcohol.

I remember being around sixteen or seventeen when a kid named George Little snuck a bottle of tequila in his backpack, I tried a swig of it to look cool. I remember gagging instantly. In retrospect, its funny to think I was fine swallowing big loads of cum, but a little alcohol was enough to make me want to puke.

"That shit was fucked up. I've done seen some fucked-up shit in my life, Pinky. Shit during the war, shit out on these streets" Lonzo shook his head as he poured a glass for himself. I had never seen this side of Lonzo, this calm, yet visibly shaken side.

"Yeah, it's been crazy." That was all I could say. I didn't know how to be in this situation. This was a man who had verbally abused me for over a year, not to mention the beating I received from his two henchmen anytime I fucked up.

"In the war, I remember being pinned down for what seemed like days. We were deep in some third world jungle, fighting a bullshit fight that had nothing to do with us." Lonzo looked down at the glass in his hand, he threw it back with one large gulp. "It wasn't like we didn't have all the water in the fucking world. It rained in the jungle almost every five fucking seconds, that pit would fill up quicker than we could drink."

I just stood there, a full glass still in my hand, seeing Kenny's face in my mind, it was enough to shoot down the sweet fire from the glass. "Jesus, fuck" I said wincing.

Lonzo never looked up from his empty glass, he stared down through his dark tinted sunglasses. I knew from experience that he was not just staring at that glass, he was staring into the horrors he had experienced.

"You try to get out and find some food, but snipers fire at you from all sides. They were trying to starve me and my men."

I pictured a young Lonzo in dirty combat gear, stuck in some deep mud pit in the jungle.

"After a few days, your friends start looking like plump turkeys on thanksgiving, all dressed up, seasoned with fear and regret." He looked over at me for the first time since we had walked into Lonzo's seventies dressed nightmare of a room. "We ate the weak, the injured, the sick." He looked back down at the empty glass.

"After two fucking weeks of being stuck in that god forsaken hell hole, we were found by a team of scouts. After seeing what we had done to survive, they took us out of that hole and threw us right into another."

To my surprise, Lonzo stood up and started walking towards me, his intentions unreadable. "The flies and maggots ate everything that we couldn't. I shit my fucking men out like they were a cheap ass greasy cheeseburger, Pinky." He stood only inches from me, his breath even worse than I remembered.

"Look at me now, Pinky. I'm some fucking pimp in Moon city. Even after the war, I'm still feeding on the weak, I'm still in that fucking hole." He sat down on the faded leather recliner that I had not noticed before. He put his face in his hands after taking his glasses off and setting them in his lap. I stood there, awkwardly. I did not know what to do or say. Did he deserve my pity?

"What did you need to talk to me about?"

He looked up at me again, only this time I could see the pain behind those piercing eyes. I pulled the crumpled letter that was now also covered in blood splatter from my jeans pocket. "The Spanish guy who did all that shit at the motel, this is a letter from him."

Lonzo unfolded the letter. He reached over for a pair of reading glasses from the side table drawer next to the recliner. I watched him read it the same as I watched Kenny, his eyes skimming over each line.

"Well, I don't have many of you mother fuckers left, guess I need to help out where I can. What do you need from me?"

He folded the letter back up and oddly stuck it in the pocket of the dark red rope he was wearing.

"Um, well maybe if you could send me some backup to look for him. He said he was close by." Lonzo looked up at me, his face blank and emotionless.

"This dude put what's his name in the fucking hospital and killed two others, almost three." He nodded at me. "You want me to send the only muscle I have protecting what's left of my investment out on some wild goose chase looking for some crazy ass Mexican?" Lonzo leaned back in the recliner, shaking his head in disapproval.

"You said you would help me" I pleaded. He turned in the chair to face the wall, then back around towards me.

"Let's be honest, Pinky. You don't make money. You come back to the house in the mornings with two, maybe three blow jobs worth of cash. That shit isn't cutting it."

Now that he had shown me a different side of himself, I guess this is where he has to show me that he's a tough guy pimp that has to make the tough guy decisions.

"Now if you were a top earner like Nicholas was, or Gilly, maybe I'd feel better about expanding my resource's to help you out. Look, I am going to help you, but you aren't getting that kind of help." He stood up shaking his head while walking slowly over to a painting of a naked black women taking a bubble bath. "I'll give you this, maybe it'll help you solve your problem when you find it."

He took the painting carefully from the wall, revealing a small grey combination locked safe. He spun the dial a few times before the loud click. One pull of the small handle revealed the safe's contents.

"Let me see" he mumbled, digging through a few stacks of hundred-dollar bills. "Here it is" he turned around holding a black pistol.

"This is a Beretta point three-eighty automatic." He slammed the safe door closed, putting the painting back in its spot. "Take this, it will solve any problem you have."

I sat my still full drink down on the side table and took hold of the pistol's handle.

"You ever shot a gun before, Pinky?" Lonzo asked, standing painfully close.

"I think I shot something similar to this when I was a teenager." A memory of my father smacking me in the back of the head came rushing in like an angry bull.

* * *

"How can someone hold a handgun like such a little homo? You cannot shoot straight worth a fuck. Is everything about you gay? You cannot even hit a fucking backyard target from six feet away?"

A hard smack that landed close to the back of my neck made me stumble forward, dropping my father's handgun in the dirt. "Stupid fuck!" he screamed as he kicked me before I could get back up.

"That piece cost more than your fucking life. You're just going to let it sit there in the fucking dirt like it's nothing? Unlike you, that fucking gun is capable of something in this life."

I quickly reached for the gun but another kick in the ass sent me forward again, my face sliding in the dirt.

"You are the worst mistake anyone could ever make, you fucking little queer." A hard stomp on the back of my head meant lights out.

* * *

"It's loaded, so don't be sticking in your ass or nothing like that" Lonzo said, slapping my back. I was relieved when he stepped away. The smell of his breath lingered, but it was roses and lavender compared to standing next to him. "The serial number has been scratched out, that way if the cops find the piece, they aren't linking the shit back to me" Lonzo added as he walked over to pour himself another drink. His voice became a distant echo as I thought about the money in that safe. All that money earned off the backs of the whores like myself. The money he kept locked away for himself, a nest egg that would allow Lonzo to call it quits any time he wanted.

The anger boiled. We were given fucking table scraps, not enough to even afford places of our own. This son of a bitch kept us needing him like we were fucking addicts.

"Lonzo!" I screamed as loud as I could.

As soon as he turned around, he knew what was coming to him, his face wide with the fear of death. I aimed the gun at his head.

"What the fuck do you think you're going to do, Pinky? You going to just shoot me after I take the time to talk to AND help you? You bitches just take and take until there's nothing left, bunch of dick sucking vultures." He threw his reading glasses to the ground in anger.

"Open the fucking safe again!" I demanded, pointing the gun in the direction of the painting.

Lonzo did not move an inch, he stood there burning holes through me. I had never seen him so angry. "You're a fucking low-level faggot. You're not even a cute faggot, Pinky. You're fucking nothing without me."

I squeezed the gun tightly, I kept the sight dead locked on his big ass

76

forehead. "Open the fucking safe Lonzo, I won't ask you again." He grew angrier when he realized I was not paying any mind to his insults.

He stomped his white loafer hard on the shag rug. "Where the fuck are you going to go? Are you going to take my money and run, Pinky? You going to fuck and run?"

He stomped his foot even harder. "I give you a roof over your head and a toilet to drain your pussy in, and this is what you do to repay me? You point my own gun at me?" He stepped forward, I took aim at his leg. A warning shot would show that I was serious. "Shoot ,bitch!" Lonzo screamed as he stepped even closer.

I closed my eyes and squeezed the trigger...

Click...click

"Fuck!" I said aloud looking down at the apparently unloaded handgun.

"You dumb fuck, you think I am going to let you see all that money in my fucking safe and then just hand you a loaded gun? Fuck, you might be dumber than you look, Pinky." Lonzo laughed as he stepped for and snatched the gun from my hand in a single swipe.

CRACK!

Lonzo used the gun like a pair of brass knuckles to my jaw. I fell backwards, my head smacking a coffee table littered with an assortment of meth and coke. "You want to bite the fucking hand that feeds you, Pinky? You want to fuck over Lonzo the mutha-fucking great?" Another strike with the gun rocked me.

"You dumb fucks going to come in now or what? I see your feet under the fucking door."

The penthouse door opened and there stood the twins, their hands covered in blood. "You get those bodies taken care of?" Lonzo asked them while he panted heavily. They both nodded their heads like obedient robots.

"Were you just going to stand outside the door while this punk ass bitch shot me?" he asked, pointing the empty gun.

"No sir, we knew you had it all under control" one of them answered, scratching their head.

"Well, regardless. Pinky here done went and fucked up. He betrayed me in the worst way possible. I need you boys to take Pinky down to the river and dump his ass after you slit his throat. Do you think you two can handle such an easy task?" Lonzo asked, lowering the gun.

The twins looked at each other and nodded. "We just dumped the other bodies in the river, boss. Do you think it's smart to go back there again tonight?"

Lonzo looked up at the slightly taller twin, astounded. "Wow, I am impressed with that question, Walt. You must be the smartest brother huh? I have spent years wondering who the dumber fuck was, now you just showed me."

The twins looked at each other confused, like they didn't know if Lonzo was complimenting them or being insulting.

"Um, thanks boss" the one he called Walt responded.

"Get this pink fuck out of my fucking sight. Take him to a different spot than the one you used to dump the others, genius."

The twins lifted me effortlessly off the floor. "Sure thing boss" Walt said, nodding.

This was it, I was going to be killed like a fucking dog and thrown in the nastiest fucking river in the state. I wouldn't find the Spaniard or help my brother.

"Should we put him in the trunk?" I heard one of the twins ask the other.

"I don't know. I mean, he's not dead like the others were. Maybe he wants to ride in the back." I could not help but shake my head at how dumb these two really were.

"I just don't want to mess up and get sent back to that scary hospital. Mr. Lonzo said we would never have to go back there as long as we did a good job." The twin must have been referring to the Moon City state mental facility. If that was the case, it would explain a lot about these two.

"Are you going to behave?" the one who is name I didn't know asked, grabbing my hair and turning my head towards him.

"Yeah, I'll behave" I answered trying to nod.

"Put him in the back seat. He said he would behave. If he doesn't, we can just snap his neck before we get to the river." They nodded at one another before tossing me like a rag doll into the back seat of Lonzo's Cadillac.

As soon as my face hit the leather seat, I started looking around for anything I could use against these two giant morons. I could outrun them if I made a break for it when we get to the river, but if by chance they are somehow faster than me, I am shit out of luck. They both got in the front seat, which seemed odd. In most cases, you would assume that one of them would sit in the back to make sure I didn't try anything funny, but these two clearly had a mental disadvantage. The car rumbled as the engine started up. I needed to think and do it fast, these two would have no problem killing me when we got to our destination. I looked down in the floor, nothing but some crumbs and a rolled-up magazine with some actor's face on it.

"Shit!" I whispered under my breath.

"Are we going to get food before or after we kill the pink guy?" the twin in the passenger seat asked his brother.

"We can't very well stop the car at a drive-thru this late at night with a guy in the backseat we plan to kill. Think about it, dummy" Walt responded, tapping his pointer finger on his head.

The dumber twin turned around to look at me "We're stopping to get something to eat after we kill you. We would stop now, but we don't think that you're going to behave in the drive-thru."

He stared at me waiting for a response, his eyes glazed over like a donut, his mouth slightly hanging open, obviously forgetting to swallow his spit.

"I mean, you all can stop whenever you want. I'll behave, I promise." I said, feeling hopeful.

"You hear that, Walt? He said he would behave. Let us stop and eat" Walt looked up into the rearview mirror, immediately locking eyes with me. He didn't seem to have the confused child like look that his brother had, his was far more aware.

"He's lying to you, Bobby. He won't behave. You have to stop believing things people say. Not everyone is as honest with you as I am, buddy." As soon as I heard the nick name 'buddy' being used between two brothers, my

79

heart sank.

* * *

"I'll always be here for you Buddy" I told Keith while we rode in the back of the car belonging to the lady in the navy-blue sports jacket.

"You swear, Gavin?" Keith asked barely being able to hold his eyes open.

I held out my pinky finger, "I pinky promise, bud." He smiled, locking pinkies with me before falling asleep on my shoulder.

* * *

I was getting the hell out of here. I had to find the Spaniard.

"You know something Bobby. I have a brother as well."

Bobby turned all the way around in the passenger seat, almost like an excited kid ready to hear a bedtime story.

"Turn around, Bobby. We weren't told to talk to him" Walt hissed.

"Don't pay him any mind, Pinky. He's always in such a cranky mood" Bobby snickered as he stuck his tongue out at his brother. "What's your brother's name?" Bobby asked smiling like a big dumb saint Bernard.

"His name is Keith. He's a really great guy from what I've heard. I haven't talked to him in a long time."

Bobby's smile faded just a tad. "Well why haven't you talked to him in a long time? Did you two get in a big fight or something?" The confused look on his face was hard not to smile at.

"I have not spoken to him since I was eighteen, he was a lot younger. He and I never fought, we always looked out for each other."

Bobby looked even more confused now. "So, if you two never got in a fight, why don't you talk to each other?"

I looked over out the window, should I tell this retard the one secret that I had never uttered to anyone? Would it better my chances of getting out of here? It was worth a shot.

"My brother and I didn't have the greatest life growing up. My dad was a vile, horrible monster." I looked out the car window as it started to rain. "After Keith and I finally got out of our house, Keith was sent to live with my mother's sister in Utah. Well since I was eighteen and my aunt was a bit of a strict old-school housewife, she felt it was best that I be out on my own."

Bobby nodded his head to show that he was still listening.

"I moved out to Utah to be closer to Keith, find some work and an apartment, but I ended up getting in trouble trying to rob a convenient store. I had never been in trouble once in my life. I got caught the one time I did something stupid."

Bobby looked confused once more "Why would you rob a store?" he asked dumbfounded.

I looked for a moment out the car window, past the now heavy rain.

"We're almost to the river" I muttered low enough that Bobby could not hear me.

"Tell me why!" Bobby demanded. I looked at him like a disappointed parent.

"I did it because I had been living on the streets, only getting to visit Keith every so often when my aunt allowed it. Keith was about to graduate high school, and I knew that I needed a place to live if he was going to come stay with me, so I robbed the gas station hoping I would get enough to at least put down a deposit."

Bobby nodded that he understood, I kept looking out the window hoping that I could finish before we got to the dock.

"I got arrested and did two years in prison. By the time I got out. Keith had graduated high school and was off at college. My aunt wouldn't tell me where he went to school." I put my head down as my heart sank even lower, the more I thought back, the harder it became. "Keith went on to graduate college while I struggled to find someone to hire me with armed robbery on my background. I went to leave him a note in my aunt's mailbox one day and saw him through the window having a big graduation party. I knocked on the door, but my aunt answered and convinced me that Keith was better off without me and that she told him that I had been killed robbing a liquor store."

My fist's tightened and my jaw clenched, just the thought of that fucking cunt. "I realized there that maybe she was right. I mean, look at all he accomplished without me in his life. Since then, I tend to keep an eye on him from a distance. When he moves to a new house in a new city, I move to a new shelter or whore house in the same city." I started getting choked up, I fought back the tears that rested heavily in my eyes.

"Storytime is up, Pinky. We're here."

I looked out the window and down at the dock, thunder roared, and lightning lit up the night sky. I was out of time.

CHAPTER 8: THERE WAS PAIN

"The story was just getting good." Bobby complained and he pulled himself out of the passenger side door of the purple Cadillac.

"We have a job to do, dumbass. If you want a story, I'll tell you the one about the fucking idiot who didn't do as he was told and got thrown in the fucking river with a dead body." Bobby had to think for a moment if Walt was being serious.

"Get out, Pinky!" Walt demanded as he opened the back door, the rain had died down quite a bit.

"You two don't have to do this. Just tell Lonzo you killed me and I promise I'll never show my face again." I tried to reason with Walt.

"Can't be taking that chance" Walt replied as he grabbed a handful of my hair. I was dragged out of the car and onto the wet wooden dock, it creaked beneath us, the sound of water splashed against the shoreline.

"This river smells like a stripper's shit." Walt said scrunching up his nose.

"I thought you liked eating those strippers' butts, Walt?" Bobby asked putting his hands over his head to block the rain.

"I like eating their assess, Bobby. I just hate when the bitch farts while I'm doing it."

If I weren't about to be murdered, I would find this conversation hilarious.

"Do we really have to kill him, Walt? He seems like a fairly good kid" Bobby whined.

"Shut the hell up, Bobby. He's not some goddamn pet that you just take home with you. Besides, if he was, you don't know where this one has been."

I could not agree with Walt more. I wouldn't take me home either. I was down on my knees, the rain started to pick up again, it was like a cold shower on a hot summer's night.

"It's raining Walt!" cried Booby over the sound of the falling water smacking the hood of the car.

"No shit, Bobby. I can fucking see, feel, and certainly hear the fucking rain!" Walt shouted frustratingly. "Go get the blade out of the trunk!" Walt ordered.

Bobby nodded his head and reluctantly did as he was told. "Here it is Walt." Bobby handed over a butcher's knife that was big enough to slice a fucking cow in two.

"Beauty, isn't it?" Walt asked holding up the knife, "I had this puppy special made, used it years ago to chop of dear heads when we were skinning them. Now I use it to make big bodies into smaller bodies. Hell, I have used this knife to cut up the beef in that stew Lonzo has us make." Walt stared at the knife, the blade giving off a beam of light across his cheek.

Now was my chance. I reached into my sock, pulling out the straight razor I had grabbed from Kenny's aftermath.

"Walt!" screamed Bobby. But before Walt could react, I slid the razor across his giant neck. For a moment he just stood there. I almost thought I did not push hard enough, that is, until a small slit on his neck popped open. Blood gushed out too fast for Walt to put his hands up and slow it down.

"Bob-" Walt tried reaching for his mortified brother. I could see the terror in Bobby's sad eyes. He watched as his mirror image fall to the ground gasping for a breath that would not come.

I picked up the giant butcher's knife, the handle made from a thick heavy wood, water dripped down its massive blade.

"Why? Why did you do that to my brother?"

Bobby looked up at me, there could have been tears in his big sad eyes, I couldn't tell. I plunged the knife deep into his shoulder, he screamed in agony. It took all my strength to pull it back out and plunge it in him again.

How could a person stab someone multiple times? It was exhausting.

Using my body weight, I leaned down on the handle, sending the knife deep into his face. The screaming stopped. I screamed at the top of my lungs, the rainwater almost filling my mouth. I had just killed two men. One of them did not deserve it as much as the other, but they were dead, and nothing could change that now. Searching the twins' bodies, I found a ring of random keys and their matching snub-nose revolvers. I tucked one of them in each sock. I stuffed the keys into Walt's gapping mouth, he could use them in whatever circle of hell he was in.

It took some serious work, but I managed to roll both brothers off the dock and into the now flooding river. I did not find any cash in their wallets, only pictures of them together as kids, along with their goofy looking ID cards.

"Walter and Bob Hutz" I read aloud. I dropped the cards into the water as well. I needed to get the hell out of here, this would be a difficult story to explain when the police eventually came.

I jumped in the driver's seat of the Cadillac. I could not remember the last time I had even driven a car, my useless driver's license had been expired for the last two years. The police hounded me about it at the station the night I had my run in with the Spaniard. Thinking about that night made me think about Dan if he were still alive I would have so many questions for him that would eventually lead to me having seriously mixed feelings about him. He was this person that I thought I knew, I thought I could read him, I thought he was at least honest with me. The car jumped backwards as I hit the gas.

"Fuck me!" I yelled. After getting the purple Cadillac in drive I pulled back up on the road and headed straight back the way we came.

As the rain poured down like rocks on a tin roof, I glared out the windshield trying to envision my not-so-distant future. Would I stop the Spaniard and watch my brother live happily ever after? Or would the Spaniard kill me and leave me never knowing what his next move will be. Him killing me would be enough to satisfy his taste for revenge.

"What could a pussy like you do to help anyone? Just lay down and die. Do your brother the favor you should have done years ago." My fathers voice came from the back seat. I looked up to see his face in the mirror. "All grown up with nowhere to go, I wish I could say I was surprised. Looks like all Keith needed was to get the fuck out from under your nut bag. He would be taking it in the ass in a fucking crack house if he had followed you." My father threw

85

his head back in laughter. The rearview mirror shattered, a giant gash above my pointer finger was a painful reminder that I could be stopped at any time. I was not some superhero. I wasn't an avenging angel. I was a cheap, gay male prostitute who had nothing in this world.

"You are nothing" my fathers voice said laughing as it faded away. I gripped the steering wheel and took a deep breath, I was not going to let the ghost of that piece of shit haunt my mind, I wasn't going to let it slow me down.

The sun started coming up over the gang tagged buildings. The light sent all the rats back into hiding, their fat wet bodies scurried quicky back into the sewers. A black night quickly becomes a dull and gray day in a matter of minutes.

Lonzo's car rumbled down the empty streets, the smell of burnt oil and smoke seeped through the cracked windows. Today was the day I put an end to the Spaniard. I was going to empty whatever bullets remained in these two revolvers into his fucking skull. I now had the rusty taste of blood in the back of my throat, I had felt the rush that comes over a man when he kills another, a great white shark on the hunt.

I parked the Cadillac about a block away from Lonzo's whore house, the sound of that engine would certainly draw attention. Peering over an old wooden fence behind what was once Freddy's Deli, I could see an overgrown yard with old, rusted refrigerators tipped on their sides, the smell of decaying stray cats dulled my senses. Beyond Freddy's former backyard, I could see Lonzo's house, the house that I had spent so many nights being treated like a piece of fucking rump roast, while the prime rib sat up in the penthouse sucking black cock.

My anger grew and grew. I was not angry from the mistreatment, I had grown use to that long ago. What angered me was the thought that Lonzo thought he had taken care of the problem that was Gavin White, this prick had no idea that I was just a block away, sitting in the bushes like a crazed madman. I checked the two revolvers that I had tucked into my left and right sock. One had four shots left, the other just two. I put all the brass tinted bullets into one gun. I looked down at the remaining handgun, it was not going to kill anyone, but it would come in handy. I jumped over the fence and into the refrigerator graveyard. After hopping the next fence, I landed in the old movie theater parking lot, blades of grass had fought its way threw the cracks in the blacktop.

"What the hell?" I asked looking over at the ringing payphone that sat on the wall just a few feet from me. I slowly made my way over to it, could this be some kind of drug dealers drop off point? Did I get caught up in some kind of sting operation? I lifted the phone off the receiver and put it to my ear. There were a few moments of silence, slight breathing could be heard on the other end.

"Are you going to hang around all day? Or are you going to come over and hangout with me, pink boy?" I almost dropped the phone at the sound of the Spaniards voice. "You've been hopping around through backyards like a ninja. Are you a ninja now, Gavin?"

I looked around the building close to the theater, he was watching every move I made the moment I pulled up.

"I do not think you're going to have much luck finding me like that. You keep looking over at that whore house like there's someone in there you don't like very much. Do you want to go in take care of some unfinished business? If so, let me help you." The Spaniard waited for me to respond.

"Leave my brother alone. He did nothing to you and shouldn't have to pay for what I've done." I wanted to rip the phone from the wall and smash this mother fuckers head in with it.

"The side entrance to the house is unlocked, some of your fellow prostitutes left from it this morning. The little pimp fellow is all alone. I'm not sure which room he's in now." The Spaniard was ignoring my plea.

"Did you hear me, you stupid fuck? I said leave my brother alone. This is between you and I. If you go anywhere near my brother or his family, I swear to God I will reach down your throat and pull out your fucking heart!" I screamed into the phone before I started violently smacking it against the brick wall. I put the beat to shit phone back to my ear.

"Do you feel better after that, my guy? You beat up a helpless phone. I hope you're not angry at me my friend, I am only trying to help you in this time of need."

I looked around again, I wanted to find this mother fucker more than anything in the world. "Where the fuck are you?! Let us get this shit over with!" Feeling lightheaded, I had to remind myself to take a breath.

"Go and take care of your pimp guy, then come back to this phone and I will call you and tell you where I can be found. After you do what you plan to do with that fully loaded snub nose in your pants, you may have earned the right to know. You agree, mi amigo?" I turned to look at Lonzo's house. If killing Lonzo was all I had to do to end this fucking easter egg hunt, then so be it.

I slowly opened the side door that led directly into the kitchen of the whore house. The place was as filthy as always, the familiar smell of Lonzo's beef stew oddly made my mouth water. I could hear the faint sound of rats scurrying beneath the old floor. I crept into the downstairs living room, no sign of Lonzo. The stairs creaked under my feet as I pulled myself forward using the handrail. As I reached the top, I could see our bedroom door opened at the end of the hall. A shadow danced around the walls. I pulled the loaded gun from my pants. I was going to have to sneak past the room and who ever was in it to get up the stairs to Lonzo's penthouse. I preferred no one else to have to die in Lonzo's name, but if they tried to stop me, I would do what I needed.

The door was only slightly opened, I could see a slim figure dancing in circles through the crack. The image of Kenny dancing naked and covered in blood came to my mind. The floor creaked loudly as I took another step closer.

"Who's there? Fuck off and mind your own goddamn business!" It was the voice of Lonzo coming from the room. It was him in there dancing around. I pushed the door open with the revolver and walked calmly around the corner.

"Pinky?" Lonzo asked surprised, but his look when he saw me was nothing compared to the look I had when I saw him.

"This isn't what it looks like, Pinky. It's the meth and coke" I stood there hearing the voice of a skinny black pimp with a pencil hanging out the end of his dick.

"What in the fuck are you doing with a pencil up your dick hole?" I asked, not being able to believe I had to ask someone such a question.

He looked down at the pencil that was now bobbing up and down with his every movement like he was stunned to see it there. "Oh, fuck. I didn't realize that was there. It's just that crazy shit you do when you're fucked up." He pulled the pencil out, his eyes rolled back like it was getting him off. I noticed the pencil had been sharpened at the end. "I guess I do some weird shit when I'm high." He laughed awkwardly as he grabbed his blue robe from Jordans former bed.

"Is that one of the twins' guns, Pinky?" he asked, realizing that I was aiming at him.

"It was" I said with a half smile.

His once piercing eyes now filled with fear, he knew there was no one to save him, he knew the gun was loaded this time.

"Do you still want help finding that Mexican guy? I can help you find him, Pinky. I got connections that can find anybody." he grasped for straws. "I can help you. I didn't mean for the twins to kill you, they were going to just rough you up a bit. I was only joking about them killing you, Pinky."

He begged and begged, it was kind of pathetic seeing this once battle hardened solider being reduced to a sniveling pile of dog shit. "You want the money in the safe? I got you. I'll go get it for you right now my dude."

He went to walk past, I pulled the trigger catching him in the hip. "What the fuck!" he screamed in pain, dark colored blood ran down the side of his leg, staining his white robe.

"Do not fucking do this, Pinky! I fucking made you mother fucker!" His voice grew angry. "I will come back and put my boot up your ass you fucking gay bitch!" He took a step forward only for me to pull the trigger again. The gun shot echoed, I pictured the Spaniard hearing it. My second shot caught him in the stomach. He dropped to his knees, groaning in agony, the bullet lodged in his gut like a broken bottle of hot sauce.

"You need to get me to a hospital, Pinky. You have to help me."

A giant puddle of blood formed around him like a red shadow. This mother fucker deserved pain, he deserved worse.

"Please, Pinky, I'm fucking dying" He reached a bloody hand up to me from the floor. I aimed the gun directly at his forehead, the shot sent chunks of skull and brain exploding like a roman candle. I walked up the stairs to Lonzo's penthouse, I needed to make sure no one else was here.

When I opened the door, I was stunned by an overpowering odor. When I saw what Lonzo had lying on his bed, the source of the pungent odor became obvious.

"Jesus fucking Christ!" I gagged while using my shirt to cover my nose. On Lonzo's bed lay the decomposing corpse of a man who looked to be in his early twenties. Muddy footprints covered the purple shag rug. The guy looked like he had been dead for a few weeks, his body was starting to liquefy.

As I walked closer, I noticed he was dressed in women's lingerie, his rotting genitals hung loosely from the side of the dark pink panties. A handful of sharpened pencils were crudely stabbed deep in his face. By the looks of it Lonzo had dug this poor guy up and had his way with the corpse, I assumed with the pencil still inserted up his dick.

"What in the fuck was wrong with you Lonzo?" I asked shaking my head continuing to look around the room. A set of keys caught my eye, one of these unlocked the shed out back, maybe I could get a can of gas and burn this place to the fucking ground.

I thought about the money in the safe, all that money that Lonzo had stolen from us. I knew that it would take time that I did not have trying to get it out of the wall. The others would be returning soon, and I didn't want to be standing over Lonzo's dead body when they did. I walked back down to the first floor, not worrying about being quite was a relief.

"The basement!" I said to myself loudly. The one place that was forbidden to all of us, a thick metal door with an even thicker padlock. I grabbed the keys from my pocket, one of these had to fit this lock. I looked around, time was a crippling anxiety. After trying a few keys, I found one that made the giant lock pop open. The big steel door creaked and moaned as I turned and pulled on the handle. I pictured a big, long table with huge bags of cocaine, even the cook station that produced the endless amounts of meth that was handed out to each and every one of us daily. The old light switch at the top of the stairs made the dark, gray, concrete floor light up under fluorescent tubes. The rats and cock roaches raced on another to a hiding spot.

"Hello?" I called down, hoping for no response. I was met with dead silence. I slowly made my way down enough where I could see the layout of the basement. The ceiling was lined with dimly lit lights, the cobwebs and dust hung low enough to get caught in your hair. There was no Meth lab, no tables lined with Scarface amounts of cocaine, just a row of dog kennels on the back wall.

"What in the hell could you possibly keep in those?" I asked as if Lonzo was standing at my side. I kept going until my feet met the concrete. I now noticed a few meat hooks hanging above a work bench, a work bench covered in small piles of bone and blood. Was Lonzo running underground slaughterhouse? Was he selling dog meat?

I walked over to the kennels expecting to see a few scared to death dogs cowering in the corners. As soon as I saw what was in the kennels, I dropped down to my knees. Cowering in the corner of the dog kennel was no animal, it was only the worst thing I had ever seen in my entire miserable life.

"Please don't leave me." A helpless hand reached out for me from the back of the cage. I grabbed the cage door and shook it with all I had. It just rattled loudly, not budging an inch.

"Who did this to you?" I asked as my heart raced so fast that it made my veins feel as if they were pumping out acid.

"How did you get in here?" I asked leaning closer to see the little girls face.

"The two big men that look the same put me here." The little girl's voice was frail and weak.

"I'm going to get you out of here sweetie, I promise." I looked around for anything I could use, the cage had a smaller model of the padlock from the door.

"The keys!" I shouted; the frightened girl darted closer to the back of the cage.

"I'm sorry, sweetie. I didn't mean to scare you."

I started shoving keys in the small slit on the bottom of the padlock, none of them were working.

"One of the big men put them in his pocket last night." My stomach hit rock bottom, just like the keys had at the bottom of the river.

91

"I'll find another way, I promise. Just hang in there."

I wish I could see her better, I wish she weren't afraid of me. She used the darkness in the back of the cage as her personal security blanket. I ran over to the work bench, a blood covered hammer rested on a pile of crushed bone.

"Cover your ears honey, this may be loud."

I smacked the lock, a spark flew back in my face. "Fuck!" I groaned after my seventh or eighth strike. I dropped the hammer on the ground, it bounced once and then landed with a hard thud.

"This will work" I said bringing back one of the big meat hooks. The little girl moved a little closer to the door, I could see hope filling up her saddened eyes. "Come on you son of a…"

CRACK!

The lock snapped off after one hard pry.

"Come on, lets get you out of there." I opened the door, reaching my hand deep into the darkness. "Take my hand sweetie, it's okay."

I tried to sound as assuring as I could. The little girl never reached out, she just sat there staring at me. "Take my hand, I'm not going to hurt you!"

I began to get frustrated, I was running out of time, if I had any left at this point.

"I can't grab your hand, sir" the little girl replied like she was about to cry.

"Why not sweetie?" I asked looking back into the cage.

"I don't have anything to grab your hand with." She held her arms out into the light. Little nubs wrapped in bloody brown wax paper took the place of her hands.

"What? What did they do to you, sweetie?" I asked lightly grabbing at her arms.

"They said that the grown-ups upstairs had to eat."

I could feel my stomach do a backflip, the smell of beef stew made its way down the steps to fill my nostrils with sickening dread. I ran over to the bottom of the steps, out of sight from the little girl. I vomited what was chunks of her flesh.

"Why the fuck?!" I cried out at the top of my lungs.

"There were more of us a few days ago." I turned to see the little girl peaking

92

out of the Kennel.

"Where did they take you from?" I asked wiping the vomit from my mouth. The little girl looked around the room, she stared blankly at the horrors she had already grown accustomed to.

"Mommy and I were living on the streets in an old car. They took us and some of the other street people. They promised to feed us." The girl's long tangled blonde hair covered most of the sadness painted on her face. Her clothes were dirty and old, her little arms hung there at her waist.

"Are you the only one left?" I asked looking around at the other kennels. She turned and looked at them as well, she turned back around and nodded her head.

"The big men hurt my mommy before they cut her up by the table. They ripped off her clothes, she screamed for them to let me go." In an instant I could feel the tears run down my face. I had never felt this kind of sadness before. How could anyone do this to this helpless child? What kind of fucking monster?

"Is Lonzo still here? Maybe it's the twins" I heard chatter between two people in the kitchen.

"Fuck!" I whispered to myself as I ran over next to the little girl.

"What's your name, sweetie?" I asked hugging her tightly, the smell of piss and shit smacked me like a falling piano.

"It's Lacy, and I think I turned six just a few days ago" she said, pushing the hair out of her face. Her emerald green eyes looked up at me like a scared kitten.

"I'm getting us out of here Lacy. I'm going to get you to a doctor who will make you feel so much better." She nodded at me with as much of a smile as she could.

I carefully scooped her up, her little arms squeezed tightly around my neck.

"I think you might need a nice bath when you get to the doctors" I joked with her. I climbed the steps hoping that the two voices I heard had made their way upstairs and were busy finding a brain splattered Lonzo. We reached the very top of the steps, the sun light shown through the half opened steel door.

"We're almost out of heren Lacy" I whispered in her ear.

With Lacy's little head pulled tightly to my chest, I peaked through the door to make sure the coast was clear. The second I could confirm, we were shooting straight for the kitchen door.

"Then who the fuck did It, Adam!?"

I heard shouting coming from the second floor. I raced to the kitchen door, flinging it open so fucking hard that the little glass window shattered in the frame.

"We're out of here, Lacy!" I said, smiling. Her arms tightened around my neck with what I hoped was excitement. "Let's get you to the doctor."

I looked both ways before running across the street, not that I needed to with the small number of cars that came up and down this road. When we reached the other side, all I could feel was happiness. This little girl was going to be ok. She was going to need serious therapy for the rest of her life, but she was going to fucking live. As we made out way down the street Lacy started getting heavier and heavier. Fuck, I was so weak. The adrenaline was wearing off.

"Okay, sweetie. Do you think you could walk with me the rest of the way?" I sat her down and brushed myself off.

"Yeah, I'm good.

A loud crack that sounded like a bullwhip being snapped stopped Lacy in the middle of her sentence.

"What the hell was that?" I said, laughing nervously. I tried to not sound freaked out. "Lacy?" I turned and watched her little body hit the sidewalk, the sunlight shined through a hole where part of her face was just seconds ago.

"Lacy!" I screamed falling next to her lifeless body.

"Who fucking did this!?" I screamed as the tears started to flow again. "Who fucking did this?" I grabbed her head and held it to my chest. "Who fucking did this?" I screamed a third time. The sound of a ringing payphone down the empty street answered my question.

CHAPTER 9: LOOK AWAY

"What did you do!?" was the first thing I screamed into the blue receiver. I had hoped it was good and loud from my end. The phone was being held together by duct tape.

"Did you just shoot a little fucking girl!? She had nothing to do with this, you fucking cock sucker!" Part of me really didn't want to hear his answer, there was no logical reasoning behind what he had done.

"Mr. Gavin, you must calm down if you wish to have a civilized conversation. If you blow out my eardrum, I will not be able to hear what you have to say." His coy, nonchalant attitude somehow angered me further. "Now that little girl was taking up valuable time that you do not have. You were taking her to the hospital, no?" He contradicted himself by asking a time-wasting question. He knew what I was doing.

"You knew I had to help that girl. You fucking killed an innocent child!" I screamed as loud as I could, I hoped his fucking eardrum burst.

"You are screaming again. If you keep screaming, I will just have to take this very expensive rifle and make a nasty hole in your head as well." I looked around again, he had to be somewhere close, for him to make that shot and be watching me the entire time, he could have been breathing down my neck right now.

"That child was not part of the plan, Gavin. She was a distraction that you cannot afford if you wish to save your little brother. I feel as if I did you a favor that you didn't quite deserve." Knowing what little I knew about this psychopath, he honestly believed what he was telling me. "Now forget the child. She died quick and painless, there are much worse ways to go." I shook my head without saying a word.

"Don't shake your head like that, my friend. It was for the best and you know this." I looked around once more, from the corner of my eye I saw movement, I turned back around hoping he did not notice.

"Tell me where you are like we agreed earlier" I said, feeling his eyes locked on my back.

"Gavin, you don't like to play by the rules. I said after you took care of your business to run to the payphone we had just spoken on and I would call you. You did not do this as I asked." I had enough at this point, I was done with this game of his.

"Listen to me and listen close, you foreign prick. When I find you, I'm going to kill you in the worst possible way. You are going to feel every second of pain, you will fucking scream as I cut out your ass hole and feed it to you." I slammed the phone down before he had time to respond.

I tuned with my hands raised in the air. I wanted to taunt this mother fucker. "Can you see me?!" I screamed looking towards the window I had seen the movement in. "Are you up there? Do you want to kill me? Do it!"

I looked down at Lacy's body, she deserved better. The sight of her lifeless, little body made me feel as if I had the strength of one hundred men. "I'm coming for you!" I screamed so loud it felt as if my next breath would make my throat bleed. I ran across the street, an abandoned cereal factory sat desolate, dark, and empty.

"Fucking clowns" I said kicking on the flimsy barricade where the main entrance once stood. An old, faded sign featuring a happy clown waving at you, his big red nose, his rainbow-colored afro and his signature blue and yellow clown suit. A fitting mascot for children's cereal. Underneath it read BUCKO'S SUGAR POPS "Taste the smiling difference!" A trick that I had once let suck my toes said that he worked there as a supervisor before the place went under, said the FDA had discovered the not so safe chemicals used in their child friendly cereal. Since the day I moved into Lonzo's, I hated having to look out the window and see that fucking clown waving at me from down the street. Nothing ruins a good morning sunrise like a fucking clown.

Inside, the front lobby was littered with graffiti and old employee files. The dust in the air made my nose and eyes water. The stale smell of cereal still in the air after all these years. I jogged down the main hallway, jumping over chairs and broken glass. Posters on the walls showed the evolution of the Bucko mascot, most of the posters had been vandalized by what I assumed was teenagers, due to the vast number of dicks drawn going into Bucko's mouth. One even read... SUCK MY TITS.

A smashed to bits clown awaited me at the end of the hallway. I peeked out at the main floor, hundreds of yellow Bucko's cereal boxes spread out like a vast yellow sea. The smell of wet cardboard came from a big hole in the ceiling, a mound of soggy boxes lay heaped in a pile. Rows and rows of old conveyors lined the walls, big red tubes hung from the ceiling like dead snakes. I looked up for a moment at the supervisors' office that would have been facing out towards the street. A shadow crossed past a big window used to look down on the employees like some Vietnam sweatshop.

"Is that you up there?" I called out to no reply. "I know you're up there. You're not as slick as you like to think."

Still no reply. I was truly shocked that he had not come through the door clapping his hands telling me what a great job I had done.

"You wanted me here, now I'm here. Come out and face me like a man, not some pussy on a fucking phone."

The shadow in the window stood still for a few seconds, then started moving around the room again at the same pace as before. I pulled the revolver from my pants pocket, I had three shots left before it became a useless hunk of steel.

I gripped the gun tightly in my hand and started up the steel steps, the combination of rust and time made me feel as if they would collapse under me at any moment. As I continued my ascent, the realization that the Spaniard was now fully prepared for me to come through the door. He could have that expensive instrument of death ready to take my head off. I pictured him with his feet propped up on some old desk, his high-powered rifle aimed right at the door, just waiting for me to poke my head in. Finally, I reached the top, the view of cereal boxes and factory equipment felt a mile down. Leaning against the wall next to the door I could still see the shadow moving around, the blinds not broken up enough to see all the way inside. I took a deep breath and thought about going in slow with my hands raised and the gun tucked back in my pocket, he had no intentions of just shooting me, knowing how much he liked to talk, the idea was not far-fetched.

"I see you in there. I'm going to come in unarmed. I know you have a lot you want to say to me, so I'm going to let you say it." I turned the knob slowly; the door was stiff enough that I needed to press my shoulder against it slightly to get it open.

"Welcome to a fun-tasitc world full of Bucko's sugar pops!" a creepy robotic voice greeted me.

"Fuck!" I jumped back as a six-foot-tall Bucko rocked back and forth waving at me in the dark.

"The fun never stops with Bucko!" the animatronic wiggled and danced in place. All at once I felt disappoint with a side of relief.

"Son of a bitch" I muttered, looking at the creepy ass clown.

"Have you met Bucko yet?" the Spaniard's voice called out in the darkness. I pulled the gun from my pants, aiming it at different spots in the darkness. "When you are done meeting our new friend you should join me downstairs in the break room. Its over by the big oven looking machine." I saw a small flashing red light coming from under a chair in the corner behind Bucko.

"Sorry about this. I just didn't want you barging in waving your little gun in my face. I'm sure you understand." The light started flashing as he spoke. When the Bucko animatronic finally stopped for a moment, I could hear the faint sound of static, a fucking walkie-talkie.

"By the way, I feel our conversation will go so much smoother without you're almost empty gun. Leave it by Bucko's big red shoes and meet me down here at your earliest convenience my dear friend."

That sneaky little fuck, he did this shit to get a good little laugh before he did whatever sick shit he had planned.

I tossed the gun towards Bucko. "Ask mom and dad to get our newest flavors the next time you visit your local supermarket." I wanted to put the rest of the bullets into that fucking things head.

The break room door was where the Spaniard said it was, next to a beat up industrial sized oven. I could see the sunlight lighting the room through the little rectangular window on the door.

"Come in, my friend. No sense in a closed door keeping us from reuniting!" I heard the Spaniard call out to me. This fucker knew every move I made before I even made it. I entered the room, smashed up vending machines and a few lunchroom tables remained. The Spaniard sat in a creaky rolling chair in the corner.

"Gavin, my friend, it feels like a lifetime. How have you been?" He stood from the chairs with his arms out in embrace.

"Stay the fuck away from me you sick twisted piece of shit!" I put one hand out the keep him back. When he took a step closer, the sun light hit his mutilated face. His cheek looked as if a dog had taken a bite from it.

"Don't be frightened by my appearance, old friend. This was your handy work, and you should be proud." I could only tell he was grinning because the working half of his mouth curved slightly. "I know my smile isn't what it was before, but I work with the tool the good lord above gives me." His arms still reached out for me.

"Back the fuck up. I'm here to talk about my brother, you said if I found you than he and his family would be left alone."

He nodded his head and lowered his arms in disappointment. He still wore his aviator sunglasses and his jean jacket with a popped collar, the only thing different was the meat grinded side of his face.

"Would you like to take a seat my friend?" he asked, gesturing towards one of the lunchroom tables.

"Stop calling me friend. You are no friend of mine, you child killing fuck!" I pictured Lacy's body sitting by the payphone, wild dogs had already found her.

"You are yelling again. Let us not fight on a wonderful day such as this." He gestured back towards the table. We sat down across from one another, he folded his hands and smiled again.

"Was it satisfying taking out your revenge on that dirty pimp? Was it everything you imagined it to be?" he asked, slightly leaning forward.

"It felt good, but not nearly as good as its going to feel to stomp that ugly fucking face of yours into this floor."

He leaned back and gasped at my response. "Now is there any need to resort to violence so early in our reunion? I assure you that there will be a time for violence." He put a hand softly to his mangled face.

"We humans are a fascinating species, don't you think? Our ability to feel empathy, anger, sadness, our ability to feel and understand such complex emotions is what makes us human, no?" I rolled my eyes at his pathetic attempt to be this philosophical psychopath. To me, he was a fucking nut with a fancy accent.

"This eye rolling, it is a sign of disrespect, is it not? Do you not respect my resiliency? If anything, you must respect that."

I smacked the table hard enough that if I wasn't so angry it would have really fucking hurt. "Just stop with all this shit. Try to do what you wanted to do and promise to leave my brother and his family alone."

He pulled his sunglasses down slightly, his dark brown eyes peering over top. "If I was to make a promise to you, you would trust that I would keep that promise even after I killed you?" He continued staring at me, studying my reaction.

"What reason would you have to hurt me after I was already dead? You like to show off and get a reaction out of the people you fucking take joy in tormenting. If I'm dead, who is there to give a shit about one dead family?" He attempted to smile again, he knew that I was right.

"So, I will be as honest as I have always been with you my friend. The black duffle bag next to that vending machine." He pointed towards the vending machine directly behind us. "Inside are the contents that I will use to take my revenge. If you were to take a peek inside, you would find a new tool I have been working on, it is a huge step forward in comparison to the drill I tried using on your penis."

I winced at the thought of that homemade dick mutilator I was introduced to during my and the Spaniard's first meeting. Turning in the chair I reached down and grabbed the bag by the long strap on top. I pulled it up onto the table, it rattled as it hit. I felt my stomach twisting and pulling as I slowly unzipped the duffle bag.

"What the fuck?" I asked, looking up locking eyes once more.

"What do you think?" he asked, reaching forward and pulling out his new contraption.

"It was made from your typical sex store strap on. I have replaced the giant purple dildo that was once at the end with what you would call a pocket pussy. You see here?" He laid his work down to spread open the skin-colored pocket pussy, the inside of the clit was pink and lined with little jagged pieces of metal. "I have coated the inside of the vagina with pieces of razor blades I threw in a blender." His eyebrows raised with excitement as if he were showing me his science fair project.

"I am very good with taking constructive criticism my friend, please tell me what you think of it." He lowered his glasses again, resting his chin on his fist. I looked down at his handy work, and then back up at the Spaniard.

"I think you are a sick fuck who has some creepy fascination with dick mutilation. I think you were forced to suck your uncle's cock when you were young and now have a closet hatred for the male penis."

A hard slap caught me off guard. I fell backwards from the lunchroom chair, my head thudding off the vending machine. The Spaniard got to his feet to dart over to where I had fallen. "You, ungrateful little American prick! I have not once called you an offensive name, nor have I made fun of you being a little gay boy! I expect the same respect from you!" he screamed like a marine drill instructor.

"Fucker!" I shouted as I jumped to my feet and tackled him down on the floor. I was never really a fighter. I was more of the one who constantly had his ass kicked and planned revenge that I never took. Today, I had evolved. I punched his face and head as hard as I could. Blood could be seen coming from his nose and above his right eye. I guess these bony fists could do damage when I put forth enough effort.

"Stop!" he tried to cry out, putting his hands up to block his face. His cries for mercy would not be met. I punched and punched until I could hear my knuckles breaking one by one on his bloodied forehead, his face felt like dough by that point. When I finally stood up, I could still feel the adrenaline pumping what felt like nitrous oxide through every part of my body.

"Fuck you!" I spit what little mucus I could cough up right on his battered face. I was not going to be a victim here, not this time. "Where is that gun of yours now, mother fucker? Did you leave it up stairs in the spot you shot an innocent girl from? Not so fucking tough now, are you?!" I had never felt like this, I had never felt this volcanic fire boiling beneath the surface, I was a rabid dog that had just been stabbed with a sharp stick.

"Ga..." the Spaniard went to speak. He reached his hand up to the heavens.

"Save your energy, my friend. You're going to need it." I jumped as high as I could and stomped down on his stomach, he gasped and choked.

"Why didn't you put something long and sharp at the end of that strap on? I could have used it to rip your insides out from your asshole." I picked up his anti dick instrument, then threw it on the ground next to him. He was even more unrecognizable by now, his face swollen, the blood had already started to dry and chip off like old paint.

"But no worries, I can still find a way to fuck you good and hard." Walking over to the broken vending machine I reached down inside of it and pulled out a huge shard of broken glass. "You would not like getting fucked up the ass with this would you? You are more of a dick-oriented man, right?" His jeans slid down with ease. "No underwear? This is America, my friend. We wear underwear here."

I laughed as I jumped up in the air again with both feet, landing on the Spaniard's face. His head sounded like a watermelon getting dropped on the supermarket floor.

"You are not dead yet, are you? I thought you were resilient." I spread his legs open, my hands popped like bubble-wrap, but I had not started feeling the pain of shattered knuckles just yet. I grabbed a hand full of the Spaniard's tanned dick and balls, I shoved the tip of the glass into his little piss slit, I went so deep that his cock split down the middle. I had never seen so much blood in all my life, he bled at least a gallon in the first minute.

"It's a shame you're not awake, I would love to hear you scream." He lay there motionless, his head turned to the side. I could almost see where my feet left a dent in his skull. I kept cutting, even when the glass became so slick with blood that it felt like I was sawing into my hand with every slice.

"Look at that pretty pussy!" I called out admiring my handy work. I tossed his dick meat across the room, it made a funny smacking noise against the wall. "Bet this didn't go the way you had planned" I said, running the broken glass across his throat. Not much blood came out of the gash in his neck, I guess he had already bled out.

I found a can of lighter fluid and a box of matches in the Spaniards duffel bag. I guess he had planned to burn the evidence when he was finished. After the can had been emptied all over the Spaniard's body, I struck a match, but was stopped by a ringing phone coming from the Spaniards jacket pocket. I guess it should have been obvious he had a portable phone. What else would he have used to call the payphone from inside this building?

Feeling around I found the phone on the inside pocket of the blood-soaked jean jacket. The little green screen on the front lit up with the words "Unknown caller". I had never used a portable cellular phone before, the thought of getting a phone call at home was bad enough. I could not imagine having to get one while I was out. I clicked the green button and pressed the phone to my ear.

"Hello?" said a man's voice on the other end. "I guess you're having shitty reception, so I'll call back later. You said you would call me once you left the factory. It's been over an hour, and I haven't heard anything."

"It's done" I said doing my best impression of the Spaniard, I had listened to him yap enough that it was easy.

"It's done? Oh, thank god. You have no idea how much you just did for my family. Him following me around like some fucking creep everywhere I moved was starting to worry my wife and I. I'm sure you don't care about the details. If you want to pick up the money, just meet me under the overpass we meet at a few weeks ago. Let's try for an hour from now, I have a lot to do today." There was a muffled click, I looked down at the little blank screen. The voice of my brother was no longer there.

CHAPTER 10: SWEET BROTHER OF MINE

I watched the black clouds of smoke pour from every hole of the factory, soon it would be a pile of ash. I reached into my pocket feeling the soft edge of the portable cellular phone.

"It's not possible" I said to myself as I thought back to what I had heard a few minutes ago. "Meet me under the overpass in an hour." I remember his voice, he sounded so exhilarated, so fucking relieved. The only person in this world that I would give my life for, the only person I would have gone to these lengths for. It was not hard to guess which overpass he had been referring to. The old freeman's overpass. The road was not used very much anymore, not since the road work ended as quickly as it started. The city had big plans for that part of town, it was supposed to be the future. After the city council was found guilty of embezzlement and a few other shady crimes, it all went to shit.

I waited around for a few more minutes, you would expect to hear sirens blaring a hundred miles an hour down the road when there was a giant cloud of smoke. Not in Moon City.

I took the long way around back to Lonzo's car. I did not want to be seen anywhere near the whore house. Pulling open the car door sent an agonizing pain up through my arm, my damn fingers would not move.

"Fuck!" I screamed out load as I did a quick pain dance in the middle of the street.

Finally managing to get the car door open it became an even bigger challenge to turn the key and put the damn thing in drive. "If you want your money" I could hear Keith's voice in my head again, it gave me enough to ignore any amount of physical pain in the world. On the drive I daydreamed of the many scenarios and how they would play out, none of them began or ended with a loving embrace. The back of my head started hurting when I tried to refocus on the road, vending machine did more damage than I thought.

* * *

"You just be as good as you can be. If he makes fun of, me make sure you do it too." I sat there with Keith behind the couch. We were both shaking in fear.

"Where the hell is that faggot ass son of yours, bitch?" my father shouted as he stumbled down the hallway.

Keith grabbed ahold of my hand and closed his eyes. "He'll pass out before he even finds us, buddy." I assured my scared little brother the best I could, but sadly I had spoken too soon.

"Look at what we have here. Gavin is behind the couch holding Keith's little hand. You trying to turn my boy into a faggot like you?" My father reached down grabbing a handful of my hair.

"Let me go!" I fought and screamed; it was no use when his hands started smacking my face.

"He's not going to turn out like you. He's going to be a real man, not some queer!" He threw me to the floor. I tried to crawl away, but the sting of a leather belt caught me in the back of the neck. "You know what that feels like, don't you bitch boy? Bet you have not felt this."

My father reached over to the steaming hot iron that my mother had sitting on a propped open ironing board. On the floor I could see Keith peaking around the couch, he watched in horror as my father stuck the hot iron on his fourteen-year-old brothers bare back.

* * *

I could see the overpass just up ahead, it was already dark out. The construction signs only partially blocking the massive hole in the road. I shut off the engine and walked over to the hill leading up to the main road.

I was in the wrong spot, maybe there was another overpass nearby that I hadn't thought of. Headlights coming down the road in the distance told me I was in the right spot. In the dark it looked like a dark green sports car; it was sleek and polished. The door opened and a figure steeped out.

"Is that you? You never told me your name, so I do not know what to call you." The figure approached where I sat.

"You can call me brother if you like" I stood up letting the still lit headlights catch my face.

"Gavin?" my brother said in shock.He stepped back, a thick white envelope clutched to his chest. "I thought…"

I stepped forward putting my hand up to stop him from speaking. "You thought what, Keith? You thought that fucking psychopath murdered me in that shitty old factory?"

His face still told the story that he couldn't believe that it was me that he was meeting here.

"Gavin, I swear it was never supposed to be like this. He was supposed to kill you at that motel. I didn't know he was going to murder a fucking cop and some random ass guy."

I could hear the words coming from his mouth. but looking at him. I could not fathom how much he looked like a much younger, healthier version of our father.

"You are the reason that Dan is dead? I thought he knew Dan from before." Keith looked like I had just told a joke.

"No, The Mexican guy never met Dan before that, not that I know of. He did bury his wife alive in concrete pit. I guess saying she cheated on him with the man he had just murdered made it seem more purposeful." Keith

106

chuckled like he found humor in the chaos the Spaniard had caused.

"I am the assistant district attorney. I come across these scumbags on a daily basis. One day, the chief of police called and said he had picked a guy up who hand no identity whatsoever, he was a john doe that no one had ever seen before, no arrest records, no prints on file, nothing. I talked the chief in to releasing him, he never mentioned his name or where he was from, I just knew he was grateful and owed me a favor."

My legs started shaking uncontrollably, I pushed with all my will power to keep standing.

"You followed me everywhere, Gavin. My gay male prostitute brother following me from town to town, leaving little notes, sitting outside my fucking house. You are a bad apple Gavin, and I am sorry but if I want to run for governor, I can't have people knowing about you and where we came from. It will ruin my reputation."

My legs finally buckled; I landed hard on the piles of crushed blacktop.

"Shit, are you ok? You don't look so good." Keith stepped forward extending his hand to help me up.

"Fuck off!" I swatted his hand away. Looking up at him in his nice grey suit, his boyish haircut, it made me realize more so how different the two of us had become.

"Keith, I was trying to watch over and protect you. I stayed at a distance because I knew I wasn't good enough to be in your life. I fought for you in ways that'll you'll never understand." Pathetically, I started crying.

"That lunatic you hired murdered a little girl. He shot her in the head with a fucking sniper rifle!" I cried still looking up at the boy I once protected. "This man was going to fucking kill you and your family Keith. He told me the things he would do to you!" I cried harder and harder.

"Fuck, Gavin. I told him to say that shit. I told him it would make you do whatever he asked. I even bought him that fucking gun." Keith stepped backwards rubbing his face, he leaned against the hood of his car and stared at me.

"I can't believe this, you were everything to me, Keith. You were everything." I wanted so badly to see even a little sign of the brother I once knew. It was obvious he was long gone.

"Look, Gavin. I appreciate all those little brotherly sacrifices you made for me when dad was being dad, but I have a family of my own now and I want as far away from that life as possible. You have to look at it from my point of view. I don't need my girls knowing their grandfather fucked their gay prostitute uncle years ago. What kind of father would I be if I brought you over for thanksgiving?"

If my heart was broken before, it was shattered into a million little pieces now.

"I've talked to dad about you, he says it's a good idea to keep you away." His words made my body lock up, there was no way he was telling the truth.

"Dad is dead, Keith. He and mom were killed in a fucking home invasion. Don't you remember being taken away? Don't you remember the blood?" Keith shook his head, a glimmer of pity in his eye. "Dad didn't die that night Gavin. Mom, most certainly. Dad took a bullet in the shoulder and side of his head, but it wasn't life threatening. They took us away because the police found a shoe box of child porn under his bed when they came to investigate the shooting, some of the pictures had you in them." My mind felt as if it were about to drain from my ears, the world spun around and around, it would not stop. This had to be a one of those nightmares, it just had to be. I slapped myself in the face, my bloody knuckles sounded like a bag of rocks.

"Wake up!" I screamed.

"Jesus Gavin, don't you see how fucked up you are? Years of being out on the streets really did a number on you"

I ran over and grabbed Keith by his shiny blue tie. "What did a number on me was the life I had to endure at the hands of that piece of shit you call a father! He ruined any chance I had to be normal! I took every lick for you, Keith!" Keith put his elbow into my chest and shoved me back.

"It is no one's fault that you're out on the streets sucking dick, Gavin! You were a queer long before dad ever laid a finger on you! Now here, take this and get your shit together!" Keith threw the envelope at me, it hit my leg and then fell to the dirt. "Dad has been living with us. I wasn't going to let my father rot away in some nursing home, he is a changed man. Maybe you should try it, Gavin!" I wanted to lung forward again and strangle him with that stupid fucking tie, my brother was already dead, this was nothing but a shell of a painful reminder.

"I loved you Keith, I fucking loved you so much. You were my whole world. All I have ever wanted from you was to live a good, honest life and be everything that our father wasn't!"

Keith looked me up and down, his pity was gone. "Stay the fuck away from me and my family" he growled as he took a defensive step forward. "If I see you around my house again, I'll kill you, do you understand, you fucking freak?" Keith's face was then replaced by my fathers. I was a kid again, alone in my room holding tightly to my little brother. "Goodbye, Gavin" Keith said as he got back in his car.

I sat there in my room watching my little brother get up and leave the room.

"Keith!" I cried out. He backed his car up and sped off down the dark and empty street. "Keith, please don't leave me alone... please!"

In the end I had gotten what I had always wanted... my brother was happy.

"Life has a funny way of turning out exactly the way we least expect." A voice called over from a burning trash barrel under the overpass. I looked over to see an old man bundled up in a blanket, he stuck out his hands so the fire would warm them, he had the bluest eyes I had ever seen.

About the Author

Stuart Drake Bray was born in Louisville, Kentucky On September 11th 1991. He is the Author of a handful of novellas such as 'The Heretic', 'Broken Pieces of June, 'Every Little Flaw', and 'Cotton Candy'. Stuart is also the host of "The murder shed podcast" available on all podcast streaming platforms.

You can connect with me on:

🜨 https://stuartbray96.wixsite.com/stuart-bray-books

Also by Stuart Bray

The Heretic

Ren has always been an outcast at his high-school. After an invite to a party from the most popular kids in school his life will take a very dark turn.

Every Little Flaw

Madison County was once a thriving community, but now years after the local sawmill shut down the town is in ruins. The few holdouts that reside, were to poor to leave. Now the people of Maddison County must fight to survive the drifters, and a crooked sheriff hell bent on putting the final nail in the towns coffin.

Broken Pieces Of June

June has struggled to find her place in the world, jumping from town to town, state to state. But when a strange film director shows up and offers her the deal of a life time, a staring roll in her own film... how could she possibly pass it up? only this isn't Hollywood, and though June will be playing a roll... she won't be acting. She will fight for survival in the dark and twisted world of the underground snuff film.